KAYLENE WINTER

SKYLAR

Prologue - Fifteen Years Ago

Zachary Bennett's knee rests alongside mine under the table.

Not by accident. Or coincidence.

I make a conscious decision not to move away. Sure, I could pretend it means nothing, but my choice to stay put settles agreeably inside my bones.

He's shooting his shot. Or, I'm shooting mine.

Finally.

Doesn't matter if it's the last Thursday we'll all be together. On a night where every laugh lands a little sharper because we're about to scatter to different destinations.

Tonight's about living our best law school life one last time before we go.

It's bittersweet. I'm going to miss my friends. At the same time, I've longed for this moment for years.

Duffy's, an old New Haven, Irish pub, is packed wall to wall with law students burning off unbearable pressure. Most of us wear the same uniform of hoodies layered under worn jackets. Denim rubbed pale at the knees. Scuffed boots crunching peanuts on a floor sticky with beer.

The jukebox plays classic rock songs everyone half-knows. Laughter ricochets off wood-paneled walls darkened by decades of handprints. Duffy's smells like hops and fryer oil, and is characteristically loud and insistent.

This place refuses to let us leave quietly.

Julian Hart sprawls on the bench, long legs fully stretched, one arm slung along the back. His blond hair sticks up in defiant directions. He's always been large in every sense of the word. Big man. Boisterous laugh. Ginormous opinions. Huge presence.

He pulls people into orbit without trying.

Across from him, his girlfriend, Marisol Vega rests on her forearms. Black jeans hug her long legs, a battered leather jacket is crumpled beside her. Her startling blue eyes miss nothing. Marisol arrived at Yale with intention to kick ass and never pretended otherwise.

Irving Brooks sits to my left, compact and composed, nursing his beer with thoughtful patience. Irv listens more than he speaks. He always has. He sees patterns before anyone else names them, then waits to see whether the rest of us catch up. Usually with great aplomb.

Zach's to my right, wearing his usual dark sweater, worn jeans and sneakers scuffed at the toes. His black hair falls forward, and he constantly pushes it back with two fingers without thinking. He's always calm. Even now, surrounded by noise and endings. The man carries himself like someone who understands how the world works without even trying.

As for me, I'm always trying to fit in with my cool friends. Intense and a tad neurotic, I try to disguise this fact by cultivating a polished, refined demeanor. Unfortunately, I'm rarely successful. Mostly because I have a hard time containing my expressions if I'm annoyed.

In any case, we all became best friends by accident.

First semester, first week, five of us ended up trapped in the same 1L study group by a scheduling mishap and mutual exhaustion. Torts on Monday mornings. Contracts on Tuesdays. Civ Pro looming Wednesday afternoon.

Julian filled the silence with bravado. Marisol challenged every assumption. Irving spoke once everyone else ran out of air. Zach listened. I asked questions nobody wanted to ask out loud.

Somehow, we clicked and our friendship has been the best thing about law school, at least for me.

Together the five of us have survived oral arguments and panic attacks during legal writing deadlines, We've passed course outlines back and forth with coffee rings stamped along the margins. One night during second year, the power went out in the library during a storm and we defiantly finished studying by phone light, laughing harder than the situation deserved.

Above all, we've consistently chosen each other over the grind.

These four people are my best friends for life and I love them dearly, despite their flaws.

Julian's hyper attention to detail drives me nuts. Marisol us ultra snarky when a deadline looms. Irving frustratingly disappears into thought for thirty minutes then returns with brilliant clarity to leave us all in the dust. Zach's tedious steadiness, no matter how stressful the situation, is hard to live up to.

No matter what, they're my de facto family.

I look around at all of them while my knee stays molded to Zach's.

I don't move. He doesn't either.

Julian lifts his glass first. "Last Thursday. After this, we're doomed to a life of full-time adulting."

"*Pretending* to be adults." Marisol clinks her glass to his with deliberate ceremony.

Irving lifts his beer in a small salute. "Speak for yourself."

Zach and I hold our beers up as well. The familiar laughter of my best friends knocks something in my chest. This moment between this exact constellation of people will never exist again.

"One more round." Julian thumps the table, rattling our drinks. "We need a toast to whatever comes next."

The bartender knows us well and passes us fresh pints of Guinness without asking. Foam settles. Condensation runs down the glass. I take a sip and let the bitter taste coat my tongue.

Conversation drifts easily, as it always does with us. Tonight, mostly focused on the dread of bar exam prep. Apartments. New jobs. The quiet terror of being set loose in the world without a syllabus.

Julian and Marisol speak about New York with confidence, certain they'll thrive there as a couple. Zach will be there too, even if he hasn't fully committed yet. Irving's future points west, tech deals and startups in San Francisco and Silicon Valley. Seattle waits for me, quieter and farther away, chosen on purpose.

Zach's knee angles a fraction harder against mine.

"You're quiet," he says, low enough for only me.

"Taking it in."

"Smart."

I smile. "Habit."

His gaze lingers, not heated or hungry. Present. Steady. Giving nothing away. Attention generous enough to blur lines without crossing any.

Admittedly, even if I can't relate, his demeanor is one of the things I adore most about him. How careful he is. Deliberate.

It's also maddening. I'm never quite sure where I stand.

I think of growing up in my parents' house, filled with drama and voices sharpened like scythes during the constant fights. Money made everything louder. Eventually, lawyers turned love into leverage and promises broke under scrutiny. During their divorce, I learned early how easily permanence fractures.

I'm returning home to Seattle because I want to do things differently. After the bar, I'll start at Finney Cooper, a prestigious law firm with a great client base. I plan to prove family law doesn't have to mean scorched earth or victories tallied in damage. It can mean protecting children and keeping something beautiful intact when possible.

Ultimately, I want to be the kind of lawyer who lowers voices instead of escalating them. Who treats families as if they're worth preserving, even when they're breaking apart.

Julian slaps the table again. "We're never going to be together as students again." His grin falters for half a beat before he recovers. "We should do something memorable."

"Define memorable." Marisol arches a brow.

Irving shakes his head. "Nothing good will come of this."

"Smoke break." Julian ignores him.

Marisol squints. "None of us smoke."

"Metaphorical."

And so we all spill onto the sidewalk, breath fogging. Julian and Marisol gallop down the block, hand-in-hand, already bickering about cabs and neighborhood bars we're about to conquer. Irving lingers long enough to meet my eyes, a quiet smile passing between me then Zach before he turns and follows them without further comment.

The door to Duffy's swings shut behind us, muting the noise. The quiet is strangely jarring.

"I'm sad this is ending." I turn toward him as we amble behind.

He nods. "Well, everything runs its course, so they say."

"Yeah, well. I hate endings." I tug my jacket closed around myself.

"Me too."

We stop under a streetlight. He faces me fully, hands in his pockets. I've known this man for three years. The emotions I've kept hidden are more dangerous tonight than ever before.

"You're going to be incredible." He smiles.

"So are you."

Silence settles between us. Weighted. Honest.

"We won't have this anymore." I drag the toe of my boot through grit on the sidewalk, watching the pale line vanish almost as soon as it appears. "Study sessions. Random dinners. Nights here at the pub."

Julian's laugh floats from farther up the block, unchecked. Marisol's gleeful cackle cuts through it. Irving lifts an arm and flags a cab without missing a beat.

"No. We won't." Zach steps closer. Enough to narrow the night to what stands between us.

I look up. His attention holds mine. Steady. Unreadable. Refusing to offer permission or retreat.

Until, a kiss lands firm and exact, stealing my breath before I can prepare for it. His hand settles at my waist. Not tentative or urgent. *Authoritative.* He holds me in place to keep me anchored.

My balance settles and my lips answer without thinking, opening and letting it deepen. My fingers twist into the fabric of his hoodie, gathering it tight. His mouth moves with mine, control loosened by restraint finally released. The years between this moment and the day we met dissolve under desire and heat.

Time stretches without permission. My body lines up with his, instinct taking over where caution usually lives.

Nothing about this is borrowed or reckless. Our kiss carries familiarity layered with something new.

Something *chosen*.

He draws back only enough to breathe. His forehead rests on my temple but his hand stays locked at my waist. His thumb nudges once. Deliberate. A signal meant to be remembered.

"Cab's here," Julian calls, snapping us back to reality.

Marisol whistles.

Zach releases me and reaches for my hand, fingers closing around mine without pause.

We jog to catch up, laughter breaking free as we reach them. Julian slings an arm around Zach's shoulders. Marisol loops her arm through mine. We pile in the cab, knees knocking, coats brushing, breath uneven. Irving scoots over to make room.

Julian names the next bar, which is fairly close. Marisol agrees. Irving nods. Once the door shuts, the driver pulls out and the city of New Haven blurs past the windows.

Zach repositions so his leg crowds mine, stupidly intentional now. His arm snakes along the back of the seat, close enough to claim space without crowding me overtly. I scoot closer, purposefully, because this could be our last chance to tilt the dynamic between us.

Heat blazes through me before thought catches up. His kiss lingers on my mouth, unresolved. Want settles deep. Certain. I've spent years managing my secret crush. Redirecting my energy to avoid detection. Filing away my attraction to Zach as something impractical.

None of my restraint holds now.

I want him with unsurprising clarity. Not as an escape. Or rebellion. Fucking Zach will be something incredible, even with distance waiting on the other side of graduation. Our lives may be heading in different directions it doesn't erase what's happening here.

It sharpens it.

Being with him tonight isn't about what comes next or where we land after bar prep or how often we'll cross paths once geography intervenes. It's about giving in to something we've both held at bay for too long.

It may be unspoken, but he knows. I know.

We'll stay out with our friends for a few hours. We'll laugh and drink and carry the night forward as friends, the way it's always been.

Later, when the noise softens and the crowds thin, he and I will slink away without any formal announcement.

No one will notice, which means no one will stop us.

Tonight's gonna end with his hands all over me.

I won't regret it for one second.

Chapter One

Fifteen Years Later

WHEN WE'RE BOTH IN town, Monday nights are ours.

Not officially. Nothing's set in actual stone.

Still, for the past decade or so, whenever our schedule's permit, Zach and I meet at the Metropolitan Grill for dinner. We've been doing it so long, the staff know us well enough to seat me in our favorite booth without asking.

I get there first. I always do.

Control is a small thing, but it's mine and I prefer to sit with back against the wall and a view of the door.

I smooth my napkin over my lap, check the time and pretend I'm not waiting.

Tonight's topic of conversation, undoubtedly, is our friends' wedding. The invitation is beautiful. Heavy paper. Embossed crest. A castle outside of Prague because of course Marisol would choose it for her Disney princess wedding. For fuck's sake, she's marrying Julian in a place with five turrets.

From my vantage point, I observe the door open.

Zach steps in. Navy jacket. No tie. A watch I once googled out of curiosity and immediately regretted when I found out it cost more than eighty grand. He pauses just long enough to clock the layout before his eyes find me.

He saunters over, unhurried.

"You're late." I lift my wine.

He eases into the booth across from me. "I'm semi on time."

"What a creative definition of punctuality." I swirl the liquid in my glass.

He adjusts his cuffs. "You've been auditing my time management skills since law school."

"I'm a born litigator." I set my wine down. "Details matter."

He glances at the bourbon in front of him, then at me. "You ordered."

"You're welcome." I'm not even a little bit ashamed at taking credit for the foresight of the overattentive restaurant staff.

His knee brushes mine when he stretches his legs out. He doesn't move.

Neither do I.

"So." He rolls the glass between his palms. "Who did you dismantle today?"

I recline. "Tech founder. Divorcing my client. He built a communication platform. Now they won't speak without counsel present."

"Poetic."

"She wants to depose his meditation instructor." I hide my grin with my hand.

He huffs a laugh. "Let me guess…"

"You'd be right."

We slip into our rhythm. Our ritual. Work is always first, it keeps the ground steady.

"I had lunch with a first-year today." I break a piece of bread in half. "He called me ma'am."

Zach's mouth curves. "You've been there fifteen years. You're allowed to terrify associates."

"I don't terrify them." My mouth drops open.

"You do." He grins. "Under the guise of mentorship."

I shake my head, smiling despite myself. "It's not my fault they think I was born a partner."

"You've been one for five years." He slices off a chunk of steak. "No small feat."

There's no teasing in his voice now.

I glance up. "Yeah, dog years."

"Earned." He eases back, fingers resting loosely around his glass. "I watched you suffer through year three when everyone else started lateraling out. I also remember year seven when things were so competitive you almost walked."

I freeze for half a second. "I wasn't serious."

"You were." He flicks his eyes to mine. "You called me from outside the building and said you were done with firm politics."

I look down at the tablecloth, tracing the weave with my fingertip. "I was exhausted. Billable hours are no joke."

"My recollection was your fury at the misogyny," he corrects, watching me steadily. "There's a difference."

I swallow.

He furrows his brow. "You stayed. Built your book. Gained credibility and won over the men who underestimated you. When the equity vote came up, no one was surprised when you made partner on your first try."

"Well," I let out a breath, "I sure was. Flabbergasted."

"You shouldn't have been." He shakes his head.

The earnestness in his voice stirs something in my chest. "You make it sound simple."

"It wasn't." His thumb moves absently along the rim of his glass. "You're not the kind of person who quits things you decide to win."

The restaurant noise fades at the edges. "I don't like to toot my own horn."

"I know." There's no performance in him now. No banter.

"Besides, you were in London that year." I try to lighten the mood. "You didn't exactly witness my day-to-day."

He inclines forward a touch, forearms resting on the table. "No, but we talked all the time and were on the phone when you found out. You read me the email as if you didn't believe it. Then you went quiet."

I remember it clearly. Sitting in my car in the garage. The fluorescent lights buzzing. My name on the memo.

"You didn't have much to say."

He nods once. "Yeah."

"Why?"

His jaw flexes before he answers. "I was so proud of you."

The words land without flourish./

"I still am," he adds, holding my gaze.

Something constricts low in my throat.

Fifteen years. Hundreds of Monday dinners. Promotions. Losses. Parents divorcing. Multi-billion-dollar deals. Clients suing. Cities transitioning.

Through all of it, he's been there. Not loudly. Not possessively. Just there.

"You're insufferable," I say without heat, because it's quite the opposite.

He lifts his glass. "No, I'm consistent."

In this moment, I realize he might be the only person who has consistently witnessed every adult version of me. The wide-eyed law student. The ambitious junior associate.

The exhausted grind of day-to-day practice. The woman in a parking garage learning she made partner. Now., a nearly-forty-year old career lawyer.

I take a sip of wine to quell the lump in my throat.

He watches me over the rim of his glass. Not invasive. Aware.

Talk moves to our parents. Mine still bitter and angry since their divorce. Convinced the other one ruined civilization. Neither one afraid to share these opinions with me at every opportunity. His are still married. Steady. The kind of happy every couple aspires to be.

"My parents taught me not to trust marriage." I scrunch up the napkin in my lap.

He turns his glass slowly in his hand. "Mine taught me not to settle, they're still like teenage sweethearts. It's cute."

I quirk an eyebrow. He shrugs.

Dessert arrives. He picks up his fork. "Change of subject. Have you booked Prague?"

It isn't *actually* a question.

"Not yet." I scoop a bite of cheesecake. "I did look at flights, though."

"Don't."

I glance up. "Excuse me?"

"My jet is a better way to go." He proclaims. "You should fly over with me."

I set my fork down. Fold my hands loosely in front of me. Fix him with my most pointed gaze. "I'm perfectly fine flying commercial."

"You won't, though."

I tilt my head. "You're eerily confident."

"I'm being practical." He meets my eyes, doesn't blink. "Besides, why wouldn't you want to hang out with me instead?"

There it is.

"You enjoy pushing me." I rest my chin on my palm.

He drums his fingers annoyingly. "I enjoy watching you pretend you don't appreciate nice gestures."

"I don't care for spectacle."

"It's transportation."

"It's *your* transportation."

His mouth curves.

The memory hits without warning.

The last night of law school. My apartment half-packed to move back to Seattle. Me lying naked on my mattress, which was still on the floor because the bed frame was dismantled.

I swallow.

Wearing only his boxer shorts, Zach stands at the foot of the mattress drinking me in. Pupils darker than I'd ever seen them.

"You're drifting." He waves his hand in front of my face.

"I'm thinking."

"About?"

"Prague."

"Liar." He adjusts and stretches his arm along the top of the booth. Relaxed. *Too* relaxed. "Say yes to the jet."

I draw back. Cross my legs. "Don't pressure me."

"You're insane. Since when is a private jet ride pressure?" He chuckles.

His shoe lightly taps mine. Not accidental.

He kneels down between my legs slowly. Methodically, his hands travel up my thighs, parting them without hesitation.

Heat coils low in my stomach. I reach for my wine to steady my hands and focus on our conversation.

"Marisol's going to make it a production." I roll my eyes. "I'm imagining a horse-drawn carriage. String quartet. Twelve-course dinner."

"You'll love every second of it and pretend otherwise." The skin around his eyes crinkles when he smiles.

I scrunch my nose. "I won't."

He arches a brow.

His mouth traces the inside of my thigh. Unhurried. Patient. Intentional. As though he has nothing else planned for the rest of his life except this.

My pulse jumps.

"So, tell the truth. Are you hesitating because it's a private jet," he narrows his eyes, "or are you afraid of being alone with me?"

I scowl at him. He doesn't look away.

"You're so arrogant."

"Noooo. *Observant.*" He holds eye contact.

Silence settles between us. Not awkward.

Charged.

We've never talked about our night of debauchery. Not once in fifteen years. Nothing.

There's been no mention of how he held my hips in place when my body tried to curl away from the intensity of what he did to me. How he made me go over again and again and again until I didn't know up from down.

My fingers close around the stem of my glass.

He notices. "Skylar..."

I blink. "Yeah?"

"Where'd you go?" he asks as if he doesn't know.

I play along. "Nowhere."

He studies me for a second longer than he should.

"Fine. I'll fly with you to Prague," I say finally.

His jaw clenches slightly. Then he smirks.

I squeeze my eyes shut at the memory of how I arched off the mattress when he devoured my pussy like I was an ice cream sundae. Every detail is infused in my soul. My hands fisting his hair. Voice gravely from crying out his name every time he made me come.

The server clears away the cheesecake we barely touched and sets the bill down.

"We'll be there for five days, unless you want to add a couple extra for sightseeing after the wedding." He reaches for the check before I can.

Wait, what?

I pout to distract him from my reaction. "You always pay."

He glances up. "Yes. I always will."

"You're so irritating."

"I'm aware." He signs the bill without looking at the total.

He devours me for hours until sunlight peeps through the curtains. Sometimes smiling up at me from between my legs, lips glistening with my release. I wonder if my unraveling was something he'd planned throughout law school and finally accomplished.

I scoot out of the booth. Zach stands and steps behind me and lifts my coat from the hook. His fingers brush the back of my neck as he places it onto my shoulders.

It's barely a touch but it burns.

Outside, the air is cool. The city buzzes around us. He walks me to my car parked up the street, even though it's unnecessary.

"How come you've never asked?" His hands are in his pockets now, watching me.

"Asked what?" I feign ignorance.

"How I felt about our night. The one after graduation."

The world narrows.

"I dunno. Because it's in the past. One and done. You didn't seem to want a repeat."

A beat.

As we approach my Mercedes, traffic moves behind him. Someone laughs from one of the balconies in the building above the street. I hold his gaze.

He stares at me, smoldering.

Zach rises from the edge of the mattress, cock in hand. Strokes himself with long pulls, forehead etched with restraint. He comes in arched spurts all over my nipples, the visual of which is permanently etched in my memory.

Zach opens my car door. Immediately, I slip inside. He closes it gently, palm lingering on the glass for half a second.

As I pull away, the ghost of his hands on my hips gives me a little thrill. I also realize he never answered me.

What's his end game? Why bring it up now?

I guess I'll find out in a few months when I'll be thirty thousand feet over the Atlantic with him. Then, five days in Prague with our best friends in a fucking castle.

This man's secretly held my heart in the palm of his hand.

It's been fifteen long years of pretending it doesn't matter.

I'm not sure I want to pretend anymore.

Chapter Two

Three Months Later

THE INVESTOR TRIP TO Dubai ends in toasts and applause.

Sunlight glares off polished steel in the conference room high above the city. Numbers are agreed to. Paper signed. Hands shaken. A photograph is taken for posterity. I hold my expression steady, nod at the right moments and allow my colleagues to believe I'm focused solely on the scale of the transaction we finally closed.

After the hoopla, I'm on my way to the elevator when my phone vibrates. Julian. It's not about the wedding, it's only a five-word text.

> Julian: Acquisition proposal. Full buy-out.

Patience prevails until I locate my driver. Once I'm settled into my seat and on my way to the private hangar, I open the Letter of Intent. It's an absurd number with numerous zeroes. The purchase price glares like a beacon. My business. Everything I've spent the past decade building. Reduced to a price.

Shiny towers whizz past the window and one thought runs on a continuous loop.

Am I in a simulation?

I should be elated thinking about valuation and the structure of this deal.

Strangely, I'm bummed. Instead of returning to Seattle, I'm rerouting to New York. Closing a transaction of this magnitude requires my immediate presence. Eye contact. Vibes. The whole thing.

I'd hoped to make Monday dinner with Sky.

We haven't seen each other since our last dinner, but we communicate nearly every day. Yesterday, she sent a photo of her desk at Finney Cooper, paper stacked in clean vertical lines, captioned with dry commentary about surviving another contentious divorce.

I sent her a photo of the skyline from Dubai, neon and impossible, accompanied by a quip about sovereign wealth fund managers behaving badly.

Everything is easy. Familiar.

Us.

I was looking forward to spending time with her. Our ritual matters more to me than most things in my life.

Without fail, when we're both in town, I show up. She shows up. No scheduling gymnastics. No calendar invites. It's understood.

For years, it's been the one place where I'm not compelled to negotiate, perform, or close. I sit. Breathe. Watch her tilt her head when she challenges me. Delight when the purple streak in her hair catches the light when she leans back in the booth.

Sky added it to her hairstyle about a decade ago after a particularly challenging year. A male associate threw her under the bus to a partner. He, in turn, chastised her for being too meek. She was devastated.

Everyone in our friend group propped her up. Encouraged her to be herself and the rest would follow.

A week later, we had our regular dinner at the Met. She showed up with a slash of bright violet framing her face. No explanation.

A declaration.

I won't allow myself to be submissive.

She's kept it ever since, I think, because it gives her the courage not to shrink. It's a slightly softer shade now, woven nearly innocuously through her dark strands. I love it because it reminds me she belongs to no one but herself.

Our last dinner before I left for Dubai isn't a comfortable memory the way most of our evenings are. It lingers in my body. Permeates my ribs when I'm alone, bringing to mind something we started and never finished.

When I told her I wanted her on my plane, she started up the usual banter but didn't blow me off. Or deflect to get out of it. Instead, she went still. No sideways comments. Nothing clever to lower the temperature between us.

The air actually realigned. Not loudly or dramatically. Her beautiful face softened. I'd only seen her loosen up this much once before. The night of graduation. Her apartment. Half-packed to move across country. Mattress on the floor. A lamp in the corner casting soft light on her skin.

Sky watched me approach with a combination of desire and confusion. She didn't retreat, though. She sank back slowly, palms flattening on the sheets behind her as she eased down.

I can still see her, spine curved like a cat. Hair fanned over the pillow. Shoulders relaxed only because she willed them to be. Her generous breasts rose and fell with each breath. Nipples darkening and taut under my stare. Thighs open enough to expose her glistening pussy.

To this day, I've never felt more trusted as when the woman I'd coveted for years exposed her most intimate parts to me.

This unexpected softness choked me up. When I lowered myself to taste Sky's pussy for the first time, I remember looking up and watching her try to hold on to control...and the moment discipline slipped and desire replaced the caution in her eyes.

I didn't rush because I knew our timing was wrong. I couldn't keep her. Instead, I had to memorize every inch. The way her stomach flexed when I tasted her honey and musk. How her fingers slid through my hair and anchored me in place.

I remember the exact mewling sound she made the first time I made her come. When she finally stopped fighting it, her head tipped back and her body opened completely. Hours blurred as I made her go over and over again.

Skylar Morgan is addictive.

Last time I saw her at the Met, as we chatted I held her gaze longer than usual. Her throat moved before she could stop it. Her fingers gripped her glass like it was going to slip off the table.

With every fiber of my being, I knew she was remembering our night. How my lips coaxed orgasm after orgasm from her body.

I also knew it wasn't the first time she'd thought about us.

If I'd had any doubts before, they were gone.

Once I've completed the sale of my company, it's time for us to make new memories.

Plural.

Going forward, I don't want one perfect night to be frozen in time while we continue to orbit around each other for the rest of our lives. I want Sky in my bed without a countdown to departure.

She's my future. Without caveats.

The fact of the matter is, I'm hopelessly in love with her. Every time she looks at me, it gives me a flicker of hope.

Recognition. Heat.

Choice.

Instead of spending time with her before the wedding, I'll be in New York, sitting in a glass office overlooking the Hudson while contemplating what my life will be if I sell. We'll talk about scale and strategic positioning. They'll talk about expansion and what my brand could become under different ownership.

Needing some advice from my best friend, I FaceTime Irving from the jet.

"You look exhausted." He peers at me through the phone sitting at his kitchen counter.

I nod. "Dubai is done. Took longer than I wanted it to."

"And?" He fills his water bottle from the tap.

I squeeze my eyes shut then open them again. "On my way out the door, Julian sent me a buy-out offer. British company. Lots of zeroes."

"Wait." He stills. The change is subtle but real. "For the whole business?"

"Yup."

He exhales through his nose. "Are you tempted?"

I can't help but sigh. "Dunno. I'm evaluating."

Irving studies me with the same look he's used since we were twenty-two. "Except, while you're contemplating the situation, you're headed straight into acquisition meetings, am I right?"

"Yup."

"Good luck, golden-boy." Irving takes a swig of water. "Now what about the wedding? Is Skylar still flying over with you or are you heading over straight from New York?"

"We'll go together. I'll fly back to Seattle the night before we're scheduled to leave."

He narrows his eyes. "Why make such a big effort? She'd totally understand the circumstances."

"I made a promise." I look out at the dark beyond the window then back at him through the screen. "Besides, it took me a long time to convince her. She's not backing out now."

He snorts. "Pull your head out of your ass, Zach."

"Excuse me?" I furrow my brow

"Ah, fuck it." A slow grin traverses his face. 'Seven hours in a jet should be enough to move two idiots forward."

I shake my head, reclining into the leather seat. "You don't know what you're talking about."

"Don't patronize. It's simple." He repositions his phone and squints at me. "You love her. She loves you. You've both been pretending otherwise since law school."

"Shut the eff up," I push back, not wanting to tip my hand just yet. "We're friends."

"You've hid behind those words for years." He lifts a brow.

I shake my head. "No. I respect our ability to maintain a platonic relationship."

"Lies." Irving tilts his head, studying me through the screen. "You've been too scared to lose her and have decided to settle for what you can get."

He isn't wrong.

"She doesn't want more," I insist.

"She doesn't want to *risk* more," he corrects, resting his elbow on the counter. 'There's a difference."

I exhale slowly. "You aren't at our dinners."

"No," he agrees with a small shrug. "Except, over the years, I've seen you two eye-fucking each other many times. You aren't exactly subtle, even when you think you're stealth."

A reluctant huff escapes me.

"Sky grew up watching her parents tear each other apart," I try to explain. "Now she dismantles marriages for a living. She's cynical. I don't think she wants long-term anything."

"No," Irving's tone softens. "I think she's waiting for a safe landing."

The word "safe" hovers between us.

"And you," he adds, angling closer to the camera, "haven't made things easy."

I stiffen.

"You've thrown your love life in her face," he continues. "You're photographed with women who have a million Instagram followers and you confess all of it to her."

"I'm not gonna sit home. I'm no martyr." I narrow my eyes.

"I'm not judging your sex life," he snarls. "I'm pointing out Sky's been watching you treat everyone else like an actual option while she's your Monday choice. *Monday.* For fuck's sake."

I go quiet.

He continues, gentler now. "Then, when she finally dates some, you critique his résumé until she breaks it off instead of telling her she deserves better."

"I don't want to overstep." I wince.

"Nah. You're protecting your access." He holds my gaze. "Having your cake. Eating it too, etc."

His words land squarely in my gut.

"She's been in love with you for years." Irving levels his tone a bit. "Do you really think she shows up to have dinner with you out of nostalgia?"

My jaw clenches. Irving's read on the situation is insanely accurate considering he has no idea what happened fifteen years ago. "I've never wanted to corner her."

"You wouldn't be cornering her." He straightens. "You'd be *choosing* her."

I inhale slowly. "She doesn't want more."

"Zachary." He arches a brow. "I've got to call this once and for all because she's important to me too. Sky hides behind friendship for safety and you give her ambiguity."

I close my eyes for a second.

"Look. Deny it all you want but know, I'm glad you're finally making a move on our girl." Irving crosses his arms. "I will warn you, don't get her hopes up if you're not gonna follow through."

A faint smile pulls at my mouth. "You have no faith."

"Since when am I religious?" he counters. "Look. Don't let her think she's optional."

I can't help but blurt, "She's not."

"Then *say* it to *her*." He throws up his hands in exasperation.

"Fine," I shout. "I'm done pretending."

Irving nods once. "Good. Because I'm tired of watching you two circle."

"This could ruin everything. She could walk away," I admit my worst fear out loud.

"Yeah," he agrees. "Or she could finally hear what she's been waiting for."

"She's *mine*," I say with certainty.

Irving smiles, slow and satisfied. "Good. Make sure she knows it."

We hang up, and the cabin falls quiet except for the steady hum of the engine. The clouds racing by my window blur into abstraction. With nothing solid enough to anchor to, I let the phone rest in my hand for a moment longer before setting it aside.

Irving's words of advice don't fade. They settle.

It's long past time to stake my claim. I've spent years convincing myself patience was noble. Restraint was respect. Giving her space was proof of understanding.

No more.

Straightening in the seat, I close my eyes for a beat to visualize Sky walking toward me on the tarmac. The wind tugs at her coat. The purple streak catches light in contrast to the gray sky. She pretends she's composed while the pulse in her forehead betrays her.

Yeah. I *know* her.

I can't wait for a safer moment.

It's time to go all-in.

Next week, by the time the wheels of my jet touch down in Prague, she won't be able to pretend she isn't mine.

Ever again.

Chapter Three

Ten Days Later

MY SUITCASE IS PACKED, zipped, and standing upright by the door.

Mocking me. Every time I walk past it.

Even my condo seems aware of what tomorrow could mean. My friendship with Zach is my most important relationship. I'm facing a long stretch of time with him alone.

On his private jet.

For me, outside of our one transgression years ago, the potential of pushing things into uncharted territory with Zach has never been an option.

Too risky.

His invitation might mean nothing. But...the way he looked at me at dinner was...different.

Even still, there's no scenario where I do something stupid to jeopardize our relationship. Not without a guarantee our friendship won't change.

As if saving me from my inner dialogue, my phone vibrates on the kitchen counter.

Prague Chaos Thread notifications ping in rapid succession.

> Julian: Final rehearsal dinner head-
> count tonight. I refuse to reorganize
> tables inside a castle.

> Irving: Just me. No plus-one. I de-
> mand seating far from any interpre-
> tive dancing.

> Marisol: There's no interpretive
> dancing.

> Zach: Wanna bet?

A smile curves before I can stop it.

Marisol attaches a schedule to the string. Thursday night is reserved for law school crew. Friday rehearsal dinner at the castle. Saturday ceremony at four followed by a reception.

I respond automatically. Confirm I'll be at the venue early. Promise to wrangle Marisol's sister if needed. Let them know it's only me for the meals.

Then Zach chimes in with:

```
Zach: Sky and I arrive at noon.
```

My heart begins to pound as my mind begins whirling again. I haven't seen Zach in weeks. The last time we were together, something shifted. I felt it under my skin.

I didn't deflect. I didn't hide. I agreed to fly to Prague with him.

Since then, we've talked and texted a bit. Trade fragments of our days. Nearly two months later, I can't help but worry there's been too much space. Space gives my brain room to draft arguments. Construct defenses. Identify risk.

Not good.

My phone rings. Marisol.

I answer and put the phone on speaker while I pace.

"Tell me you're not spiraling." Her voice is bright and suspicious all at once.

I close my eyes and sigh. "I'm not spiraling."

"Oh, you're absolutely spiraling," she counters. I hear her heels click faintly on her hardwood floors.

"We haven't seen each other." I push off the counter and walk to my bedroom. "He's been with your husband."

"And?" she prompts, impatience layered over concern.

"We won't have a Monday dinner before we leave." I lower myself onto the edge of the bed. "I don't know what's what."

She exhales slowly, understanding immediately. "So you're going straight to a runway with no reset."

"Yes."

A soft laugh leaves her. "Tragic."

"This isn't funny," I protest, staring at the suitcase near the door.

"I'm not making fun of you." The humor fades from her tone. "Are you scared you misread everything?"

"You weren't there." My fingers trace the seam of my comforter.

"I didn't need to be," she insists. "Fact of the matter is, he specifically invited you and *only* you onto his plane. He could have offered to fly all of us over, and he didn't."

"He's decisive," I murmur.

"With work," she counters, and I can almost visualize her lifting a brow.

I recline into my pillows and stare at the ceiling. Adrenaline pumps through my body and I can barely breathe. "Oh, God. What if you're right and I *did* misread the situation?"

"Sky," she soothes softly, "don't be scared he'll pull back."

"I'm not." I swallow. "I'm scared I won't."

She laughs. "It's about time you told him you need a repeat."

"Except, I don't want to ruin our Mondays." I glance out the window at the Space Needle glittering in the distance.

"For God's sake, Sky. Monday isn't sacred," she replies firmly. "It's comfortable. You're not moving forward if you stagnate in a friendship when you want more."

She has a point. However, status quo has kept me steady for years.

It's also kept me safe.

My phone vibrates on my thigh. I glance at the screen.

Zach.

"Hold on." I bolt upright.

Zach: I'll meet you at the jet at
7:30. Boeing Field. Clay Lacey Aviation.

Meet you at the jet. No car ride together. No easing in.

"He just texted," I tell Marisol.

"And?" she queries.

"He wants me to meet him at the plane." I pace a groove in my hardwood floor.

She releases a low sound. "Oh."

"Exactly."

I can already picture it. Wind tugging at my coat. Engines whirring. Zach waiting with his signature controlled, unreadable posture.

"This is going to be a catastrophic mistake," I whine, stopping in front of the mirror to check myself out.

"It could be," she agrees. "Or it could be the start of something amazing. Either way, you've both avoided this for years. At least you'll have—"

"If this goes badly," I interrupt, "I lose him."

"Sky. You don't *have* him," she replies gently.

Ouch.

"At least I have *something*," I press my palm flat on the dresser.

"No," she responds. "You don't have what you want."

Silence stretches for an uncomfortably long period of time.

"You don't want safety," she finally speaks. "You want *him*."

The truth bristles under my skin.

"True, but I don't want to make a fool of myself," I whisper.

"You won't," she replies without hesitation. "I promise."

My eyes fill with tears and I'm grateful we're not on a video call. "You can't know that."

"I know both of you, and you'll survive," she assures.

Her certainty steadies me more than it should.

"If he steps forward," she continues, "are you sure you're not gonna step back?"

I picture his face at dinner. The way his voice softened when he told me he wanted me there.

"I am. I want to explore this if he does," I answer finally.

"Good."

We transition back into logistics. Dress steaming. Timeline adjustments. How many tissues she'll need before walking down the aisle to Julian.

When we hang up, the apartment is noticeably quieter.

I open Zach's message again.

>   Meet you at the jet.

My pulse rises.

>   Me: I'll be there.

The three dots appear almost instantly.

>   Zach: I know.

I stare at the words longer than necessary.

Is he really so certain? Does he have any doubts?

It's late. I need to get some sleep, so I plug my phone into the charger, climb into bed, and turn off the lamp. The suitcase stands by the door as proof I'm not backing out.

Tomorrow, after work, I'll meet him at his jet and we'll fly to Prague together. With nothing left to buffer us.

By the time we land, I'll have my answer.

Chapter Four

The Next Evening

EVEN THOUGH I FLEW in from New York early this morning, I've been at Clay Lacey Aviation for most of the day.

Control is comforting, and this flight could change my life. Everything has to be perfect.

The industrial hangar lights cast soft halos over the polished steel of my Gulfstream, which is capable of crossing oceans without strain. The fuel trucks pulled away half hour ago. The transatlantic routing has been filed. Weather over the Atlantic clear enough for a smooth crossing.

My pilot, Magnus, is slowly and methodically walking the exterior with a flashlight, tracing lines along the fuselage, checking panels, intakes, surfaces.

Inside the cabin, catering is being arranged with quiet precision. I step into the galley and nod once to the attendant, who straightens immediately when she sees me.

Cristal is chilling for take-off. Screaming Eagle is decanting for our dinner.

Beluga caviar nests next to a basket of linen-wrapped blinis. *Crème fraîche* in porcelain. Mother-of-pearl spoons aligned beside the setup.

On the prep counter, Balik salmon has been sliced thin as silk. Oysters rest on ice with carved lemon spirals and a shallot *mignonette*. A5 wagyu steak and Maine lobster are already prepped for a final sear and butter poach after takeoff. An entire white truffle is ready to be shaved over the top.

Dinner is set up perfectly, so I move on to the aft suite.

The bed is made. Crisp white linens pulled snug enough to reflect light. A full-size gray Minky Couture blanket is folded at the foot of the bed. I smooth my palm over the fabric, noting how soft and cozy it feels. A few months ago she mentioned falling asleep wrapped in one of these on Marisol's couch.

Details matter and tonight I'm going to make it impossible for her to misunderstand my intention.

Now, all I have left to do is wait for her.

Strolling back into the forward lounge, I lower myself down in my lounger and let my shoulders sink into the soft leather. My briefcase rests near my feet. Inside, a copy of the final purchase agreement awaits my review. Two hundred pages, including exhibits, documents the transaction.

If I sign, I'll be five hundred and twelve million dollars richer.

Selling is going to change everything in my life, including my identity. Strangely, this milestone doesn't seem urgent right now. The sale can wait.

Tonight isn't about valuation.

It's about destiny. I can't wait for Sky to step through the cabin door and notice the shift in our dynamic before I even say a word. Champagne instead of Rose. Caviar instead of olives. Purpose instead of routine.

I try to gather myself by clasping my hands together and steady my breathing.

Magnus interrupts my thoughts when he places a hand on my shoulder. "She's here."

My heart rams in my chest.

"Thank you." I manage to rise without rushing.

Through the oval window I catch the sweep of headlights entering the hangar. The black sedan I sent for her rolls into position beneath the wash of overhead lights. I watch from the airstair door as the car comes to a stop. The driver exits first. Then the rear door opens.

Sky steps out into the night.

Her black trenchcoat catches a faint crosswind, hair loose around her shoulders, violet thread flashing under hangar lights. She pauses for half a second, scanning the aircraft, taking in its' scale without letting it show.

She reaches back into the car for her suitcase. Two crew members approach and intercept with quiet efficiency.

"Evening, Ms. Morgan," one greets cordially, already taking the handle from her grip.

She holds it for a beat, stubbornness flickering in her eyes. "I've got it."

"Please, ma'am. You're the guest," the attendant replies, steady and respectful, rolling it toward the cargo hold.

Sky steps back, exhales once, then turns. Her eyes land on me. A flush spreads along her cheeks before she reins it in. She straightens, lifts her chin, and approaches.

I skip down to meet her.

"Hey," I keep my tone light as I close the distance.

She stops in front of me and allows her gaze to travel slowly from my polished black boots up my tailored charcoal suit. "You look absurdly put together for someone who's been burning the candle at both ends."

"I'm *always* put together." I can't help but smile. God, I've missed her.

"Insufferable," she mutters, but affection lingers in her voice.

I don't hesitate. I pull her into me. Her body stiffens for a fraction of a second, surprised, then softens. Her arms slide around my back firmly, cheek settling against my chest.

I hold her longer than I should. When I step back, my hands remain at her waist.

"You good?" I search her face for any sign of wariness.

She nods once and her eyes flick to the plane behind me. "Yeah. I'm...fine."

"Great. Let's go," I prompt, gesturing to the plane.

She inhales slowly. "Sure. Why not climb into an absurd flying hotel at midnight?"

"You're welcome." I lean down, lips brushing her ear.

She trembles.

Inside, the cabin glows, lighting set for the red-eye. Cream leather catches ochre strips along the ceiling. Walnut trim reflects soft highlights. She pauses just inside the doorway, carefully taking in the space.

"So, this is normal for you," she murmurs.

"It's actually practical."

She turns her head slowly. "Practical. *Rigggght.*"

Ignoring her lighthearted jab, I lift the Cristal from its cradle.

"Drink?" I offer, pouring the bubbly liquid into a flute.

Seemingly unimpressed, she takes it, fingers brushing mine for half a breath before lifting the glass. Her eyes widen slightly after the first sip, then she recovers. "Who are you, and what did you do with my beer-drinking law school friend?"

"He's left the building," I wink.

Her gaze drifts to the caviar service laid out in silver and porcelain.

"Oh, come *on*." She steps closer. "I'd have been fine with a bag of Doritos."

"We've got to eat. It's a long flight."

She studies me over the rim of her flute. "Okay. Now, you're showing off."

I let my posture relax. Cool. Controlled. Sky thinks this is an ostentatious spectacle.

Little does she know it's a seduction.

We move deeper into the cabin. Her fingertips trail lightly along the back of each seat, nervous energy disguised as curiosity. Through the galley and past the cabin restrooms, we reach the aft suite. I open the door and wave her inside, following at a measured pace.

She takes in the white linens and fluffy pillows, but she gasps when she notices the soft gray Minky Couture blanket folded at the foot of the bed. She reaches for it before she can stop herself.

Sky groans as she rubs the plush, fur texture, then freezes. "Where did you get this?"

"You recognize it." I grin.

Her brows draw together. "This is Marisol's. Ohmygod, is she here?"

"No, it's just us, but you haven't stopped talking about this blanket for the past two years," I explain quietly. "I bought it for you, this goes home with you after the trip."

Her fingers remain sunk into the fabric. "I didn't realize you'd paid attention."

"I always pay attention to *you*," I answer honestly.

She looks away for a moment, blinking, then back at me.

"I can't believe this is your life," she admits. "Jets and champagne and excess."

I step a little closer, narrowing the space between us. "This flight isn't for anyone else."

"Well..." She sets the champagne flute down carefully. "You're making it hard to keep teasing you."

"I don't mind you teasing me." I wink.

The roar of the engines deepens as the crew begin final checks.

"We should sit." I hold out my hand, which is visibly shaking.

"Are you nervous?" she whispers.

I eek out a slow breath. "A little. Not about the flight."

Her lips part. Eyes widen.

If I'm not mistaken, Sky understands what I'm putting down. Or, at least, hopes...

She's bracing. Same as me.

Ahead, I hear the cabin door seal with a muted thud.

"Come on," I offer my hand, "let me show you your seat."

She nods once and steps closer, her shoulder brushing mine as we walk forward into the inevitable.

Chapter Five

A Few Minutes Later

THE ENGINES GROWL BENEATH the floor as we prepare to taxi to the runway.

He gestures to the seat beside him, a decision sending a jolt to my heart even if I pretend otherwise. The leather is buttery soft and the seat is heated. His thigh is a mere inch from mine.

Too close. Not close enough.

He drains the rest of his champagne and rests his fore-arm on the armrest between us. I do the same and the flight attendant whisks the glasses away for takeoff.

There's something about our energy tonight. It's reckless. Dangerous.

The jet turns onto the runway. My stomach seizes. Zach glances at me. I hold his gaze.

We lift.

Seattle falls into a glitter of sparkly lights and our world narrows to cabin light, vibration, and electric energy.

The crew moves stealthily. Seatbelt signs chime off once we level. The forward cabin dims further, amber sliding into something softer.

New flutes of champagne are presented. I take a sip and allow the bubbles to settle under my tongue. Caviar service is placed between us with near silent precision. Silver lid lifted. Blinis. *Crème fraîche* smooth as silk.

"You do realize," I break the silence, "most people would have offered peanuts."

He turns, glass resting between his fingers. "When will you get it through your thick head? I'm not most people. Especially to you."

My pulse skitters.

I stare at him and laugh under my breath. "You've lost perspective."

"Possibly."

He spreads *crème fraîche* over a blini, adds a measured spoonful of caviar and hands it to me without breaking eye contact.

I take it. Our fingers brush. Salt and cream dissolve in my mouth. I close my eyes for a fraction of a second before opening them again.

"This is absurdly delicious," I sigh.

"You deserve absurd." He smiles. "Always have."

I laugh nervously because...*Jesus.*

The flight attendant discreetly indicates the smaller dining table in the galley complete with white linen, candles encased in glass, and plates positioned dangerously close together.

Zach rises first, unhurried, and I follow him back as the cabin lights dim a fraction lower. We settle side by side, our shoulders nearly parallel. I can't help but wonder if the arrangement is intentionally intimate.

We talk about safe things at first. Julian's scheduling anxiety. Marisol's obsession with Disney. Irving's inability to sit through any ceremony without wry commentary.

Our knees keep touching, the contact accidental. In theory. Neither of us moves away. Every time the aircraft sways slightly, our legs brush together again, and a quiet pulse shoots through me before I can brace for it.

My senses are heightened. Hitched breath. Heat gathers fast in my core and lingers. Proximity to Zach is intoxicating, even through the layers of fabric. My body responds before my mind catches up.

I tell myself it's the plush surroundings. The champagne. The altitude.

It isn't.

Desire pools low and steady, spreading warmth through my stomach and down my spine. As if every nerve has woken at once. I'm hyperaware of the line of the faint flex of his body when he shifts. The space between us shrinking with each quiet adjustment.

This can't actually be happening. Not after years of maintaining careful distance.

My nipples are stiff to the point of painful. Wetness soaks my panties. I stare straight ahead for a moment, trying to steady myself, but the reality crowds in from every angle.

If I edge even an inch closer, our hips will align. If I turn my head, my mouth will find his shoulder.

The thought makes my pulse stutter. God, I want this man with every ounce of my being.

I swallow, trying to act composed, while my body quietly betrays me. Beneath the thrum of utter desire, one thought keeps circling.

Is this real?

Or, am I about to wake from a dream?

Dinner arrives in courses. First salmon, translucent and delicate, and oysters glistening on crushed ice. He watches me take the first bite.

"Your mind is working overtime." His eyes soften.

I can't look at him right now, I'm too worked up. "Always, it's my fatal flaw."

Wagyu follows, seared to perfection. Wine is poured. He waits until I taste it before taking his own sip.

"Did you plan all of this?" I hold my glass high and admire the deep red catching the cabin light.

He clinks his glass to mine. "Yes."

Indulgent. Excessive. Yet, he offers absolutely no apology. Or defense.

What unsettles me is the steadiness. Zach isn't showing off. He's calm. Decisive.

Next, earthy, rich truffle over lobster perfumes the air. It's heaven on earth. He leans back, studying me.

"You've gone quiet," he notes.

I risk eye contact. "I'm eating."

"Hmmm." He pours more wine.

"You haven't mentioned the acquisition," I dare to look at him again.

His jaw pivots subtly. "Tomorrow. Not tonight."

"Tonight is about...what?" My heart stutters.

He holds my gaze. ***"You."***

The word lands impactfully in my chest. I peer down at my plate to steady myself.

Moments later, the flight attendant clears dinner. Dessert replaces it. Gold-leaf chocolate soufflé in small porcelain ramekins. Champagne sorbet glistening like frost.

"You're ridiculous." My words lack bite.

Zach doesn't respond. He intently watches me lift a spoon and taste the soufflé. Rich. Dark. Warm.

He inclines closer before I register the movement. His thumb brushes the edge of my lower lip. I freeze.

"You missed some." He pierces me with a heated stare.

The pad of his thumb drags slowly across my mouth, collecting chocolate. His eyes never leave mine. Then he lifts his thumb to his own mouth and sucks it clean.

Heat detonates in my bloodstream. The cabin shrinks to the two of us alone.

"Zach," I breathe, unsteady.

He hovers, waiting. *"Yes."*

The control in his voice cracks something inside me. I don't think. I close the distance.

My mouth finds his with force I didn't know I possessed.

The kiss is not careful.

It's a full-blown collision.

One of his hands threads through my hair. The other hand finds my waist and holds me there almost as if he's been waiting years for this moment to materialize again.

I taste wine. Chocolate. Heat.

He makes a low sound in his throat, rough. Unguarded. The vibration travels straight through me. I edge into him harder, palm flat against his chest, the steady thud beneath his shirt thrums.

There's no hesitation left in me. No default to our friendly Monday ritual. No shields of teasing and banter.

Zach deepens the kiss, slower now, more deliberate. There's only breath. Heat.

Finally, we're not pretending.

When we breaks the kiss, it isn't because we want to. It's because air becomes necessary.

His forehead rests on mine. His hand remains at my waist.

"Skylar." My name sounds rough. Ragged.

My pulse pounds in my ears. "You don't get to do this and then walk it back."

"I won't. Never again."

No hesitation.

Inside this aircraft, sealed in warm light and intention, something irrevocable settles.

We're no longer orbiting.

We're falling.

Neither of us is trying to stop it.

Chapter Six

A Few Minutes Later

HER MOUTH HAS BEEN on mine long enough for the rest of the cabin to disappear.

My world's narrowed to heat, breath, and the taste of chocolate and champagne lingering on her lips.

Easing back, the reality of our situation comes into focus. Gold leaf glints under the light. Two porcelain ramekins sit abandoned between us, dessert forgotten.

For a moment I simply look at her.

Sky's lips are flushed. Her amber eyes hold the same fierce intelligence I've known for years, yet the control she wears like armor is slipping. The strand of purple hair has fallen loose along her cheek and she doesn't move to fix it.

God, she's perfection.

I press the call button on the armrest, my thumb barely making a sound. Almost instantly, the attendant appears at the doorway. She steps in on silent-soled shoes, her posture so composed it's as if discretion is stitched into her uniform. She reads the moment without a word.

"Could you clear this." I gesture at the place settings. "We won't need anything else for a while."

She nods once and moves forward, efficiently collecting plates and glasses, folding linen and extinguishing the candles. In less than a minute the table looks untouched.

Throughout, Sky's gaze drifts from my eyes to the lines of my jaw and back again, searching for the calm I reserve for every high-stakes negotiation.

When the curtain behind the attendant closes, the hush in the cabin deepens.

We're essentially alone.

I rise first. Not abruptly. Enough movement to break the spell.

I reach for hers without thinking.

She pauses a heartbeat, not from fear but from consideration. Then laces her fingers through mine. Her skin is warm and familiar. A current sparks where our hands meet.

Hot. Familiar. Electric.

Together, we move past the dining nook back to the forward lounge. The two deep-set leather seats now face the porthole windows revealing a black expanse, pinpricked only by distant stars.

I sit, and Sky allows me to guide her, but instead of taking her spot beside me, she turns and settles onto my lap. Her knees hook around my hips. The sensation of her weight on me sends a shockwave of desire through every nerve. My hands instinctively find her waist, palms gripping the gentle curve of her hip bones over the smooth fabric of her skirt.

Our lips meet, slow at first, testing the space we've finally closed. I tighten my hold, feeling the shift when she gives in completely. The kiss deepens, no hesitation left, only heat and the quiet certainty we've both been denying for years.

The jet sways in an air pocket with a gentle puff of turbulence, and she's jostled closer, breath still hot on my mouth. Her lips taste of champagne and a wave of emotion nearly overwhelms the moment.

I've wanted this for so long, I'd almost convinced myself I'd forgotten the ache.

Her fingers creep into my hair. At first tentative, then curling in with firm insistence. I trace the vertical seam of her blouse along the warmth of her back, mapping the slope of her shoulders, the small arch of her spine, every familiar angle.

She sways her hips deliberately, grinding on my hard cock. A low groan slips from me before I can swallow it. An involuntary confession of how badly I want to be naked and inside her.

Sky freezes, eyes wide, breasts rising and falling in rapid pulses. Then she rocks her hips again, slower this time. Purposeful. I tighten my hold on her waist, needing her anchored to me. The warmth of her pussy along my shaft is maddening.

With her forehead resting against my cheek, she inhales, steadying herself as she undulates. Holy fuck. This feels amazing. Imagine how it'll feel to plunge into her wet heat.

"We need to talk," she whispers, voice trembling but firm.

Reluctantly, I reposition her so I can look into her eyes.

Because she's right.

She stays seated in my lap while she searches my face the way she always does when she needs truth. "We never actually talked about that night."

Fifteen years of memory flicker behind her eyes.

"No," I concede.

Her hand hovers above my chest before her palm flattens over my heart. "I thought you wanted to forget what happened."

"I thought *you* did." I quirk a brow. "You shoved me into the friend-zone first thing the next morning."

She studies me for a long moment, absorbing my words.

We've devoted our friendship to remain silent on this subject. Dinner after dinner. Shared jokes. Shared history. Everything except the one moment which forever changed how I saw her. Maybe, how she saw me.

Her index finger lightly flicks my chest. "I was terrified everything would change."

"But, everything already had." The words come out before I can soften them.

She inhales sharply.

My hands drift slowly from her waist, along her back. I pull her closer until no space remains between us. Her heartbeat gallops almost as fast as mine.

"If we...um. If we do this, I don't want it to be another night we never speak about again," Sky murmurs into my ear.

I take her face between my palms. "Trust me. It won't be. I don't want that either."

"You sound very certain." Her eyes narrow a bit.

"I am."

She watches me carefully, looking for hesitation.

There isn't any.

Her hips rotate again. The motion almost unconscious now, and pressure between us builds until it's impossible to ignore.

Her breath stutters. "I need to know."

"Ask."

Her voice drops to a whisper. "Do you want to fuck me tonight?"

"Yes."

My affirmation lands solidly between us.

Her shoulders relax a fraction. "Zach, for me there's no going back."

"Sky, baby, there never was."

She nods and kisses me slowly this time. Not collision. *Recognition*.

Her mouth moves with mine with patience born from years of knowing each other. My hands tangle into her hair to hold her in place as I deepen our connection.

As far as I'm concerned, this entire aircraft has shrunk to the space between us.

When we part again her breathing is uneven. So is mine.

Her fingers stroke the back of my neck. "Can we move this to somewhere more private?"

"Are you sure?" I caress her cheeks with my thumbs.

She nods, unable to speak.

I stand. She doesn't climb off my lap.

Her legs tighten instinctively around my waist. I lift her and her arms drift around my shoulders as if she's done this a hundred times.

I carry her down the aisle. The forward lounge fades and the door to the aft suite closes behind us with a quiet click. Her eyes shine now with something deeper than nervousness.

Something hopeful.

Fierce.

"Tell me this is real." She nuzzles my neck.

"The real-est." I set her down and take her hands in mind.

She steps into me again, closing distance without hesitation.

For the first time in fifteen years, I'm not holding anything back.

Chapter Seven

Moments Later

THE DOOR CLICKS SHUT behind us, sending a shockwave through my chest.

Around me, every detail sharpens. The honeyed glow of the cabin lights. Subtle thrum of jet engines beneath our feet. Charcoal Minky Couture blanket draped at the bed's foot.

None of it matters. My world telescopes to Zach and only Zach.

He's breathing hard, chest rising and falling, shirt torn open from my impatient hands exposing lithe, defined muscles. His dark hair is wild and mussed where I've clawed through it. The careful mask he usually wears in public is gone.

What's left is raw, hungry. Starving. For *me*.

He takes my hands in his and a fever rush scorches my veins. My pussy aches to be filled with his cock.

I step forward once. Then again. He meets me halfway.

Our bodies collide. His mouth crashes onto mine, hot, claiming. My hands fist the ruined edges of his shirt, yanking him flush. His arms slam around my waist, hands greedy on my ass. I can't help but grind against the rigid bulge straining in his pants.

I whimper into his mouth as his tongue sweeps inside. Slick, hungry, taking everything. Our breaths mix in the charged silence, every inhale his, every exhale mine. Our hearts hammer as if the cabin might come apart.

He breaks the kiss only to drag in air. "God, Sky, I've wanted this for so fucking long."

I know exactly what he means. Fifteen years ago, we spent hours lost in tangled sheets, his mouth feasting on my pussy until I was hoarse from screaming. Shaking from orgasms that left me ruined.

He got himself off instead of fucking me. If I'm honest, all I've ever wanted is for Zach to be inside me. Hopefully now's the time.

Zach lifts me with a growl and my legs wind around his hips. His cock is thick and hot and it burrows into the soaked lace covering my pussy like a homing device. I moan, lost, hips rolling to get closer. He stumbles to the bed, falling with me on top of him.

The mattress groans and the gray blanket spills to the floor. He buries his face in my neck, breath scorching my skin.

"*Sky*," he rasps desperately.

His hands are everywhere. He hooks his fingers into my neckline and rips, tearing my silk blouse until the cool air licks my bare skin. Shrugging out of my bra, I arch into his palms as he cups my breasts, pinching and rolling my nipples, making me gasp.

"Fuck, you're so wet." He plunges a finger into my panties.

"All your fault," I manage, breathless.

His grin is dark. Wicked. "I haven't forgotten how you taste. I could devour you for hours..."

Unable to speak, I tremble, hips arching to his hand. He shreds my panties. Literally tears them off. Drags another digit through my slick, aching folds.

"Jesus, Sky..." His thumb circles my clit as if he memorized exactly how to make me come. "Fifteen years and you're still... Tonight, I need to fuck you. Feel you come on my cock. I can't restrain myself this time."

Reaching down between us, I grip his thick cock. Velvet-smooth in my grip. I stroke him, thumbing the swollen head with his pre-come. He shudders, jaw clenched.

"No more waiting," I pant, guiding him to my entrance.

He hesitates, breath shaky, eyes locked on mine. "Are you sure? I'm clean."

"I am too. I'm on the pill." I wrap my legs tighter, teasing him with a slow roll of my hips. "Shut up and fuck me."

He bites his lip and thrusts in, slow and deep, splitting me open. I cry out, clutching his back, nails raking down as he fills me, stretching and claiming and perfect. He holds still, cheek aligned with mine, both of us caught in the shock of finally—*finally*— this being more than a fantasy.

"You're fucking *unreal*," he groans. "God, I'm not gonna last."

"Don't care." I rock up to meet him, greedy for more. "All I need is for you to give it to me. Hard. Everything you have."

Zach starts to move, long and deep. The blunt head of his cock glides along my sweet, internal spot. My body clamps around him firmly, hips meeting every thrust. My whole world narrows to the musky smell of his skin and the sensation of fullness. The slap of skin on skin.

His mouth latches on my nipple, biting, sucking, tongue swirling. I writhe in his lap and grind my clit along the base of his cock, lost in the heat and the rhythm and the years of wanting. His hand fists in my hair, pulling me down as he takes me harder.

"Touch yourself, Sky," he orders roughly.

I reach down to my clit and rub it in slick circles. "God, Zach, don't stop—"

He's relentless. Hips snapping. Cock pounding into me until I'm wailing. Every inch of me is on fire.

"I want you to come all over my cock." His teeth graze my collarbone. "Soak me."

Pleasure coils forcefully. I'm close. So fucking close.

I rub my clit faster and I shatter around him. My pussy squeezes his shaft as my vision whites out.

"Fuck, Skylar," he snarls as his orgasm tears through him and he floods me.

Through our aftershocks, he holds me tightly as our bodies fuse. We collapse together, tangled. Skin slick. Breaths ragged. His cock softens but he stays inside me and I savor the connection. The pulsing afterglow. Sticky heat trickling down my thigh.

He lifts his head to pepper soft kisses on my mouth, throat, the point of my chin. "Don't think about sleeping. We're nowhere near being done. I want you screaming for me all night. I plan to taste you and fuck you until you can't remember your name."

"Well, damn." I laugh, still dazed. "It's either all or nothing, I guess."

He rolls us so we're side by side and I'm sprawled against his chest. "Promise. You're mine tonight. Tomorrow. For however long you'll have me."

"Careful what you wish for." I kiss his nose and let the truth settle in our bones.

His hand coasts down and slips between my thighs, teasing through our combined mess pooling there. A fresh wave of hunger builds. Sharp. Insistent. Zach's cock twitches, hardening again with impossible speed.

His hooded eyes meet mine. "You ready to go again?"

"Um..." Giggling, I bite his bottom lip. "No reason to stop now."

Outside, the jet streaks through the ink-black sky on the way to Prague.

In here, time resets itself.

Zach and I don't waste another second.

Chapter Eight

ZACHARY

A Couple Hours Later

Sky's breath quivers against my lips.

Her body is tangled with mine and another hot, insistent surge of want stirs in my veins.

I take a second to admire her. The dim cabin light turns her skin into molten honey, every inch glowing and impossibly inviting. Her hair, wild from my hands, spills over her shoulder. Her cheeks are flushed. Lips swollen from my kisses. Eyes dazed with pleasure.

There's nothing in this world I want more than her.

No one else has ever come close.

God, her body. I've dreamed about it for more than a decade. Replayed every detail of our hookup fifteen years ago. Those long, elegant legs. The subtle strength in her thighs. Curve of her waist. Sweet dip of her hips.

Her breasts are perfect in my palms, nipples already rigid and begging for my mouth again. Freckles are scattered like secrets over her shoulders and chest. And her fucking smile. Sly. Knowing.

She owns me and always has.

I cant my hips so she knows how hard my cock is for her.

Sky grins. "Seriously? Three times and you're not done?"

"Not by a fucking mile," I growl and flip us so she's beneath me, hair fanned on the pillows.

I drink her in, gluttonous for every detail. The spark in her amber eyes is always a little wicked. Her mouth is plush, sinful, made for sucking my cock and biting and whispering the filthiest things I've ever heard when I fuck her.

From this point forward, I'm gonna worship her for a lifetime and it will never be enough.

My hands roam her soft, satin-smooth skin. She's fire and elegance. Strength and vulnerability. So alive under my hands it makes my chest ache.

I kiss my way down, memorizing every inch. Taking her taut nipple between my lips, I suck hard and she arches into me. I want to mark her everywhere, let the whole world see she belongs to me.

My mouth trails lower, following the salt and sweetness of Sky's scent. I breath in the faint citrus and vanilla of her perfume, the scent of our sex on her flesh.

When I reach her thighs, I pause. Her beautiful pussy is swollen with arousal, clit distended and pulsing. My come glistens through her folds. Her body is open and wrecked from fucking me.

Somehow, Sky's even more perfect now.

Undone and *mine*.

"You have no idea how many nights I've jerked off thinking about how you look right now." I spread her wide, admiring her. "You're the sexiest fucking woman on the planet, Sky. I could die between your legs and be happy."

Her lips part, a breathless little sound escapes. "Prove it."

I drag my tongue through her slit, slow and deep, tasting the mix of us.

She gasps, hips jerking, hands flying to my shoulders. "Zach—oh my God—"

"We taste so fucking good. I could stay here forever."

I nudge her legs wider, anchoring her with my palms as I lick every drop. Bury my face in her pussy until there's nothing left but raw pleasure and the sound of her begging for relief. My tongue circles her clit, then flicks it. I suck, then sink two fingers inside, curling to ruthlessly stimulate her spongy bundle of nerves.

Sky's wild now. Her hips grind against my mouth. Nails cut into my scalp. Her voice breaks on my name. "Don't stop— Fuck, Zach, don't you dare stop—"

I devour her, licking and sucking and plunging my fingers deep until she's a writhing mess. Her thighs tremble on either side of my head, her body bows off the mattress. When she comes, her whole body clenches. Pussy spasming around my fingers as a long, shattered moan tears from her throat.

She's still shaking when I dive back in, licking her through it, sucking on her clit until she crests again, hips bucking helplessly.

She sobs out my name, breathless. "I can't— Zach, I *can't*—"

"You can and you will." I lap at the mess I've made. "You *love* it when I eat your pussy."

I keep going. Tongue, fingers, mouth, until she's spent and limp. A beautiful, trembling ruin. Sky's chest rises and falls fast, eyes rolled back with a lazy, blissed smile curving her lips. She literally glows and I let myself bask in the sheer miracle of her.

Kissing my way up her belly, I claim every inch as mine. When I reach her mouth, I don't hesitate, I kiss her deep, letting her taste the wet, musky fusion. She moans into my mouth, greedily sucking my tongue as if she can't get enough.

"You're filthy and you're mine." I nip at her bottom lip.

She laughs as her hands slide down my chest, tracing my abs, then lower. When her fingers wrap around my cock, I nearly black out. I'm so incredibly aroused, I nearly lose my shit.

Sky eases down my body and looks at me, wonder in her eyes. I take a second to savor the visual of her between my thighs, glossy lips hovering above my shaft as her gaze burns into me.

In this moment I'm sure. I'm the only person she's ever wanted.

She pushes me back, eyes dark with hunger. Her hair falls around her face as she takes my cock in her hand, stroking from base to tip.

She licks the head, eyes locked on mine. "You want me suck your cock?"

"God, yeah," I groan. "I want to fuck your hot, wet mouth."

Her lips wrap tight around my shaft, tongue swirling around the head. I fist the sheets, fighting the urge to propel down her throat. She alternates between sucking hard and licking my shaft, hollowing her cheeks then working me with her hand. Every noise, every obscene slurp, goes straight to my core.

"God, Sky, you're gonna make me come," I warn.

"I'll swallow another time." She pulls off with a naughty smirk. "Tonight, I want all of your come inside me."

I yank her up so she's straddling me, my cock barely breaching her soaked entrance. She reaches down to guide me inside. The moment I sink into her, we both gasp. Even after multiple rounds, it's like the first time all over again.

Skylar Morgan was made for me.

I cup her breasts and thumb her nipples as she starts to ride me. Slow at first, rolling her hips, then picking up the pace. Her hands grip my upper arms, head thrown back, hair tumbling down. The sight is pure sin. Sky's ample tits in my palms as she rides my cock, mouth open in ecstasy.

Pinching her nipples, I tug and roll them, sending little shocks of pleasure through her. I watch her lose herself and transform into a goddess taking what she wants from me. Owning her pleasure.

"Yes, baby," I urge. "Take everything. I want to watch you come."

She bends down, kissing me hard, biting my lip as her hips stutter. Her pussy flutters and clenches my shaft. "Zach, I'm so close."

"Get yourself there. Milk my cock."

She shatters, hips jerking, pussy spasming around me. With one more deep surge I spurt inside her again. Holding her close as we ride every last wave together.

Eventually, we collapse into my favorite position. Her head on my chest, my hands stroking her back. Neither of us speaks for a long moment. The cabin is filled with the sound of our heartbeats, the hum of the jet and the scent of sweat and sex permeating the air.

I kiss her hairline and something settles inside me.

"You better get used to this." I tuck her closer. "I'm not going anywhere, Sky. Not ever again."

She's utterly spent but manages, "Good. I don't want you to."

Moments later, we drift off, the world outside forgotten.

Promises of forever made at thirty thousand feet.

Chapter Nine

The Next Morning

MORNING ARRIVES LIKE A tide easing back from the shore of my body.

There's only warmth layering through muscles aching in the most pleasant way.

I lie still beneath the sheets, eyes closed, breathing in the faint scent of linen mingled with the lingering trace of Zach on my skin. My body has been deliciously used. Hips tender. Thighs pleasantly sore. Lips still sensitive from the hours of kisses. A bit of beard rash.

When I stretch beneath the covers, a soft sound escapes my lips, unintentional, but entirely fitting.

God.

I've never felt so content.

Not even close.

Images from last night flicker through my mind. Snapshots of ecstasy. The weight of his body pressing down on mine. How his deep voice rolled over me when he called out my name over and over. Our laughter bubbling as we collapsed into pillows, swearing we should sleep.

We didn't.

Finally, my eyes flicker open. Soft morning light filters through the small oval window beside the bed, bathing the cabin in a pale glow, replacing the deep blue-black of night. The atmosphere in the cabin is strangely quiet.

Still. No engine vibrations.

My hand pats the mattress next to me, fingers brushing the cool sheets.

An empty space.

I roll onto my side and blink more fully awake. I hear faint movements in the cabin beyond. Something sliding shut. Soft footsteps.

Zach.

The thought of him sends a slow ripple of heat through my core. My body remembers every moment of last night vividly, as if the years apart sharpened my memory instead of dulling it. The delicious evidence of our activities radiates throughout my core. A warm, heady, delicious soreness.

Four times.

A quiet laugh escapes as I push myself upright to nestle in the pillows.

Four times.

I've never had sex four times in one night.

I'm already hoping for a fifth.

The thought warms my cheeks.

The suite door swings open. Zach steps inside, a tray balanced in his hands. For a heartbeat, I forget how to breathe. He's barefoot, wearing nothing but loose charcoal pajama bottoms hanging low on his hips. His chest is bare, muscles rippling enticingly as he approaches.

He's devastatingly handsome.

Maddeningly pleased with himself.

"Morning." A playful smirk dances on his lips.

I glance at him, then at the tray, and back again. "You're kidding."

He sets the tray on the small table beside the bed. Fresh fruit glistens in a bowl, croissants nestle on a folded linen napkin, soft scrambled eggs steam invitingly. Two cups of espresso and a small pitcher of orange juice complete the spread.

The aroma makes my stomach rumble, awakening my senses.

"Breakfast," he says, as if it's the most natural thing in the world to wake up on a private jet to breakfast in bed served by my shirtless best friend.

I narrow my eyes at him. "The plane isn't moving."

"No." He leans on the wall and watches me with a teasing glint.

"When did we land?"

Zach shrugs. "About three hours ago."

Three. Hours.

I stare at him, mortification flooding my senses. "You let me sleep for three hours? What happened to the crew?"

"Don't worry about it. You needed some rest. I wore you out, it was the least I could do." His expression remains unfazed.

"Zach," I pout. "You should have woken me."

He pushes off the wall and sits beside me on the edge of the bed, the mattress dipping under his weight. His hand instinctively smooths the blanket over my legs, a gesture so tender a lump nearly forms in my throat.

"Nah. You looked peaceful."

He reaches for a croissant and tears it in half, offering me the larger piece. Our fingers brush, and the contact sparks an electric shiver. Neither of us comments on it, but we don't pull away either.

I take a bite and close my eyes in sheer enjoyment.

"Okay," I moan around the pastry, "this is criminally good."

He watches me eat with a look on his face suspiciously resembling contentment.

"You're staring," I grab the cup of espresso to hide my red cheeks.

"Well, you're glowing."

I choke on my drink, coughing. "Pretty sure it's your fault."

"Yeah." The smug smile returns. "You seemed...open to the experience."

I laugh softly, relaxing back into the pillows. The movement pulls the blanket lower, and his hand instinctively reaches out to tug it back up again, fingertips brushing along my stomach.

His hand lingers a moment longer than necessary.

"So," I carefully sip my coffee, "what's the plan?"

"For?" He raises an eyebrow.

I roll my eyes like he's an idiot. "For walking into a castle full of our best friends after what we did last night."

"Ah." Understanding flickers in his eyes.

"Yes. *Ah*."

He nestles back next to me, one arm draped casually along the headboard. "I say we walk in together. I'm pretty sure they've been waiting for us to pull our heads out of our asses."

"*Hmmm*. The throw-it-in-your-face strategy?" I cross my arms in front of me.

"It's solid."

I study his face, searching for any hint of apprehension. "You're very calm about this."

"I'm still enjoying the bubble." His thumb traces slow circles on my thigh.

"The bubble?"

"The part where the world doesn't know anything yet." His gaze flickers around the suite, taking in our clothes scattered all over the floor.

More evidence of our wild night.

My cheeks flush. "Pretty sure the bubble popped hours ago."

He kisses my shoulder, breath warm and tantalizing against my skin. "You sure?"

"You're impossible." My fingers trace the warm line of muscle along his arm.

"To resist." He stares into my eyes and winks.

I playfully shove him. "Don't be so fucking arrogant."

"Too late." His playful tone sends bolts of electricity through my entire body.

Sighing, I reach for a piece of fruit to try to redirect my focus. "We should get ready. They're probably already wondering where we are."

"You know," his hand skims my leg again, "we could stay here a little longer."

I shake my head. "We can't skip the wedding festivities you flew me across the ocean to attend."

"Worth a try." His mouth curves, amusement dances in his eyes.

I shake my head, cheesing despite myself. Then, unable to resist, I tilt my head to kiss him lightly.

"Finish breakfast," I whisper. "Then we face reality."

He kisses me back like he has all the time in the world. "Reality can wait five more minutes."

Honestly, I'm starting to agree.

Zach's fingers continue to tease circles of fire along my thigh, pulling me deeper into the moment. The warmth between us is palpable, and as I look into his eyes, I see a mix of desire and mischief.

"You know, we really *should* take our time," I suggest, my voice dropping to a sultry whisper, lips brushing along his ear. "After all, we have a few days before the wedding."

He chuckles. "Now, who's tempting who, Skylar."

"Me," I reply naughtily. "I *want* to tempt you."

He grins and suddenly the air is infused with erotic tension. "What do you have in mind?"

I consider the question for a moment, my gaze drifting down to where his pajama bottoms hang low on his hips, the outline of his growing arousal barely concealed.

I bite my lip. "I should show you just how much I appreciate breakfast."

"Oh?" He raises an eyebrow, devilish glint in his eyes. "How do you plan to show said appreciation?"

With a smirk, I allow the blanket to slip, exposing my breasts to him completely. I watch as his breath catches, gaze locked with an intensity that ignites my skin.

"I have my ways," I torment, heart racing with excitement.

His eyes darken and dilate. "You're playing a dangerous game."

"Maybe," I lick my lips. "Somehow, I think you're up for the challenge."

He grins, a predatory gleam in his eyes as he eases closer. "Oh, I definitely am."

I melt into him, fingers sliding into his hair, pulling him closer. The kiss deepens, turning ravenous as we both give in to the passion radiating between us. He slants his hips along mine, allowing me to feel the thick ridge of his cock.

"God, you're insatiable," he whispers, voice low and thick with need.

I smirk. "You started it."

He laughs throatily. "Oh, I'll finish it, trust me."

In one swift movement, he pulls the blanket aside and scoots me onto his lap, my back flush with his chest.

"Yeah, this is good." He reclines back on the headrest and yanks his pajama bottoms down.

I settle back. His cock pokes up between my legs, poised at my entrance.

"God, you're breathtaking." He kisses my neck and spreads my legs over his thighs. "Watch this," he commands as he fists his cock and taps it on my clit, teasing me mercilessly. "I'm gonna feed it into you."

With a firm thrust, he pushes up and I'm mesmerized by the visual of his cock disappearing inside me. My entire body clenches when he's fully seated. The connection ignites an emotion I can't put a name to.

"Yeah, Sky," he encourages, his grip on my hips constricting as he thrusts deeper.

His fingers move with expert precision, rubbing my clit as he continues to pump into me, each movement sending waves of pleasure. Tension coils tighter in my belly.

"Zach," I moan. "I'm so close."

"Let go for me," he urges. "I want you to think about what we're doing every minute of today."

I surrender to the pleasure, my body trembling as I detonate.

"Oh, God!" I cry out

"Fuck yeah," he groans, spilling inside me.

We're both breathless, enveloped in the aftershocks. I collapse anchored to him, savoring the warmth of his body as we slowly come down from our high.

"Reality can definitely wait a little longer," I mumble.

He chuckles softly before gently kissing my shoulder. "I agree."

Chapter Ten

A Few Hours Later

After the most decadent sexual experience of my life, Sky and I arrived early afternoon.

Together, which our friends expected.

Nobody knows what happened on the plane—yet. We were provided with separate rooms. Her room is down the hall from mine. I nearly spoke up, but Sky stopped me. She doesn't want our news to overshadow the wedding, which kinda makes sense.

I'll play along for now, but I'm not relegating myself to the shadows when it comes to her.

I can be patient for a few days. Not longer.

I'm waiting for her in the gallery above the entry to this ridiculous castle, which runs the length of the east wing. I watch the activity below while footsteps echo faintly from the corridor behind me.

Sky appears. The navy dress she's wearing is dark and follows the shape of her waist before falling smoothly to her knees. The fabric shifts in quiet folds as she moves. As always, she's elegant, but not formal enough to appear ceremonial.

Then I notice the heels. They make her legs, which were wrapped around me eight hours ago, look incredible. The memory of how she cried out my name in the cabin of the jet makes me hard.

"You clean up well." I give her the once-over when she stops in front of me.

This ignites a spark of amusement. "Careful, Zach. Someone might think you're flirting."

"Dangerous rumor."

Stone walls rise on either side of the grand staircase descending toward the dining hall. Lanterns cast warm pools of light on the masonry, smooth from centuries of footsteps. Voices drift upward through the stairwell in soft layers, echoing along the stone before fading into the quiet above us.

I have to admit, it's regal and princess-y, which is exactly Marisol's vibe.

Sky walks one step ahead, her manicured hand trailing along the cool stone railing as we move downward. When we arrived earlier, Marisol whisked her to pull her into whatever private rituals brides require before a wedding weekend begins.

I was quickly claimed by Julian and Irving, who insisted I needed to "see the place properly," which apparently meant a tour of the bar followed by a lengthy discussion about music for the reception over whiskey.

Now those separate currents are flowing back together.

Irving bounds down the stairs behind me. Sky pauses and glances back. I force my attention to the scene below before my moony expression gives anything away.

Irving, who misses nothing, inclines forward. "Subtle."

"I'm admiring the architecture," I reply without turning around.

He snorts.

Sky waits for us at the bottom of the staircase. The lantern light catches the violet streak in her hair for a brief moment before it melds back into the darker strands. Our eyes meet again and a flicker of awareness passes between us.

She knows exactly what I'm thinking.

I'm pretty sure she's thinking it too.

Sadly, we have other obligations tonight. The doors to the dining hall are already open. Accompanied by the sound of laughter and the clink of glasses. Julian and Marisol are waiting for us.

Once we walk through the ornate archway, I'm delighted to discover it's exactly what I pictured.

A long, wooden table stretches almost the entire length of the hall beneath dark timber beams blackened with age. Candles flicker down the center beside bowls of flowers and decanted bottles of wine. Tall windows line one wall, their glass reflecting the movement inside while the countryside beyond fades into the night.

Julian stands near the fireplace, talking animatedly with one of the staff members.

"Symmetry matters," he insists.

Marisol amusedly watches the exchange with a glass of wine in her hand.

She notices us first. "There you are."

Julian turns immediately. "Finally."

Irving has already drifted to the sideboard, studying the line of wine bottles with the focus of a man about to make an important life decision.

A member of the staff appears and gestures politely. "Dinner is ready."

We all move to take our places. Chairs scrape the stone floor as everyone takes their places. I take the seat directly across from Sky, because it's the safest option to ensure I keep my hands to myself.

She settles into her seat, smoothing her napkin on her lap as the first course arrives. A server sets a wide ceramic bowl in front of each of us, steam curling upward into the candlelight. *Bramboračka*, he explains, is potato soup thick with root vegetables, mushrooms, and marjoram. The smell alone is incredible.

"Okay," Sky lifts her spoon and tastes it, closing her eyes briefly, "I'm sold."

The second course is *pečená kachna*. Slow-roasted duck, skin crisp and dark with caraway seeds. Braised red cabbage glows deep crimson beside thick slices of potato immersed in rich gravy.

Conversation flows as everyone digs in. Stories overlap. Glasses refill. Irving launches into a description of the band's rehearsal earlier in the afternoon while Marisol tries unsuccessfully to keep Julian from reorganizing tomorrow's seating arrangements again.

Sky listens intently, one elbow resting near her wine glass. Every few minutes, her eyes flick back to mine.

Quick. Careful. Electric.

Svíčková, the next dish arrives. Braised beef sirloin in a creamy root vegetable sauce, garnished with cranberry and whipped cream. Bread dumplings are arranged neatly along the side.

My focus is hardly on the food. Sky looks incredible. From the way she tucks her hair behind her ear when she laughs to the faint flush lingering along her collarbone. Our eyes meet again. She holds my gaze this time. Then her foot slides forward under and brushes mine.

I freeze.

She pulls it back immediately and reaches for her wine, pretending nothing happened.

"Zach." Irving's voice snaps me back. "You're staring."

Sky coughs into her napkin.

"I'm admiring the *architecture*." I raise an eyebrow.

Irving glances at the beams overhead. "Again? You seem to be quite taken with this castle."

Sky's heel connects sharply with my shin. I almost smile.

Dinner continues in warm waves of conversation as *Vepřo-knedlo-zelo*, the final savory dish arrives. Roasted pork with sauerkraut and bread dumplings.

Wine flows. Stories stretch. Sky keeps looking at me the same way I'm looking at her. Remembering exactly what we were doing last night and this morning. Planning how and where we're going to do it again.

Her foot finds mine again. This time it lingers. Then it retreats.

I glance up and she's turned toward Marisol, nodding along to something about tomorrow's schedule. She glances over.

The smallest smile appears. Just for me.

Patience.

The word passes between us without a sound, hidden beneath the easy noise of old friends and full glasses of wine. On the surface nothing has changed. Sky chattering animatedly. Me pretending not to stare.

Once this dinner ends and the castle corridors fall quiet, none of the logistics matter.

Not the band. Rehearsal dinner.

Or the seating chart.

Most certainly not the bedroom assigned to me.

Chapter Eleven

The Next Morning

MORNING WASHES OVER THE stone walls.

This place is an indulgence of luxuries.

Half-asleep, I lie still in the expansive, ornate bed.

Beside me is Zach.

I can't help but smile. The jet seduction wasn't a one-off. Last night proved it when he tapped on my door after everyone went to bed.

The line we'd etched between us for years has been forever and permanently crossed.

Turning my head, I take in the sight of him. Zach isn't just handsome, he's breathtakingly perfect. Sculpted by artisans with a chiseled jaw and confidence to command any room. Morning light dances on his chest, highlighting every taut muscle. Tousled hair hinting at the wildness of last night—my fingers to blame. One arm is tucked beneath the pillow, the other draped lengthwise, fingers brushing me as if he wants to be sure I don't leave his side.

The sheet has slipped low on his hips, revealing his half-erect cock bobbing on his belly. I swallow hard.

Even when he's sound asleep, the man's not finished with me.

My body remembers every touch. How, for the past couple of nights, he's claimed me as if I were his entire world. I stretch beneath the sheets, reveling in the delicious, lingering ache. A reminder of the pleasure we've shared. Over and over.

I probably should be thinking about my maid-of-honor duties for the day ahead. Spa appointments. Final fitting. Luncheon with Marisol, her sister, mom, and future mother-in-law.

Instead, the truth hits me like a prizefighter.

I'm in love with Zach Bennett.

The realization is both terrifying and exhilarating as I admire every inch of his body.

Two nights in, and I'm already fantasizing about more. If this wedding weekend didn't come with responsibilities, I'd be more than happy to stay locked in this room for a week. Maybe more.

My pussy clenches sending shivers through my core. My body twitches, disrupting the mattress. Zach stirs, his brow furrowing before his eyes flutter open and land on me.

His yawn is followed by a wickedly sexy smile. "Good morning."

"Morning." I don't bother averting my ogling eyes.

He studies me with a mix of curiosity and heat. "How long have you been...admiring me?"

"Long enough to confirm your cock is still in good, working order," I joke, my heart racing at the sight of it thickening in front of me.

He laughs, rolling onto his side to face me fully. The sheet drifts off altogether and my breath hitches when he fists his cock and smears the glistening moisture along his crown.

The sight of this man gripping himself sends a rush of heat coursing through me.

"You're terrible at subtle, Sky," he smirks.

"You're the one all ripped and sexy." I bite my lip. "Sue me."

"Touché." His eyes glint with mischief.

Propping myself on one elbow, I let my fingers dance lightly along the warm line of his muscles. "I realized something."

"Sounds dangerous." He continues to stroke his cock.

I allow my finger to trail lower down his ab muscles. "For years, I told myself we were just friends."

"And now?"

"And now," I draw out, "I know I was kidding myself about what I really want."

He raises an eyebrow, intrigued. "How so?"

"God, you're enjoying this." I roll my eyes

"Immensely."

I shake my head, laughter bubbling up. "Well, this wedding weekend is turning into an incredible inconvenience."

"You think?" Amusement dances in his gaze.

"Yeah." I nod. "All these important rituals are getting in the way of what I'd really rather be doing."

He leans in so our noses are almost touching. "Tell me, Sky, what would you prefer to be doing? I promise I'll try to make it happen."

"Riding your cock," I whisper, the final word heavy with promise.

"That might be the best idea I've ever heard."

Before I can respond, he shifts closer. "Sky, if you skip the spa, do you think anyone would notice?"

I giggle. "Uh, yeah. Marisol will send a search party."

"Worth it." His eyes darken with desire.

Unable to resist, I brush my lips to his, still mesmerized at the sight of him slowly stroking himself. His hand moves quicker now, and he tilts his head back in pleasure. My mouth goes dry at the sight of him and the power he wields without a word.

Before I fully succumb to temptation, I pull back. "As much as I want to, Marisol's my best friend."

"You know," his gaze never leaves mine. "You still have half an hour before you need to leave."

A soft groan escapes me. "This is how I end up late."

"Totally worth it," he promises.

As I look into his eyes, I know he might be right.

Chapter Twelve

Early Afternoon

OLD TOWN PRAGUE IS bustling.

The cobblestones under our feet shine faintly from the morning rain. The narrow streets weave between buildings older than I can comprehend. Towers rise at odd angles above the rooftops, Gothic spires cut into a pale-blue sky while church bells somewhere in the distance mark the hour.

Tourists wander in loose clusters, cameras pointed at the Astronomical Clock while locals slip around them with the easy confidence of people who know every crooked alley by heart. Café doors stand open and the smell of coffee drifts into the street alongside the unmistakable scent of Pilsner.

Julian walks beside me, hands in the pockets of his jacket, looking suspiciously relaxed for a man whose wedding rehearsal is set to take place in a few hours.

"You realize," Irving steps around a delivery cart, "this is the most respectable bachelor party I've ever attended."

Julian snorts. "It's *not* a bachelor party."

"It's a pub crawl," Irving replies. "Same concept. No strippers."

Fred, Julian's father, laughs from behind us. "Not everything requires strippers."

"Yeah, vastly overrated." Marisol's father, Jose, shakes his head slowly.

The five of us move through the winding streets together, following Julian's confident navigation to our first stop. He's no doubt spent hours researching and mapping this route out. We turn onto a narrow street lined with tall, pastel buildings and stop outside a pub with dark wooden doors and a carved sign hanging above it.

U Tři Růží.

"Here we go." Julian pushes the door open.

The smell of fresh beer hits immediately.

Inside, the pub is dim and warm. Wood beams hang overhead and long tables are crowded with locals already deep into early-afternoon conversations. A chalkboard near the bar lists the house lager.

Tank beer.

Julian raises his hand to the bartender. "Five."

The glasses arrive seconds later. Tall. Golden. Foam rising perfectly to the rim.

"*Na zdraví.*" Jose lifts his glass.

Fred translates, "To health."

We clink glasses. The first sip is cold and smooth, indicating why the Czech Republic takes brewing seriously.

"Delicious." Julian is smug. "The perfect start to our pub crawl."

"You're marrying the woman of your dreams tomorrow," Irving ignores him, "yet you've probably spent more time researching this non-bachelor party than you did planning the wedding."

"Balance." Julian remains unapologetic.

We finish the round and wander back into the streets. The afternoon stretches comfortably as we make our way through a few pubs dabbled between Gothic arches and Renaissance facades. The Astronomical Clock chimes as we cross the square.

We duck into another bar a few streets over, this one quieter and darker. The walls are lined with framed photographs and old beer advertisements. Another round appears.

The conversation maneuvers easily the way it does with men who've known each other long enough to skip introductions, fathers included. Inevitably, the teasing Julian should have known it was coming begins.

"Seventeen years." Jose leans back in his chair. "You've been dating Marisol *seventeen* years."

Julian raises an eyebrow. "Happily, of course."

"You *finally* decided to marry my daughter."

Fred laughs into his beer.

"Don't forget the babies," Jose adds. "Twelve years old now, yes?"

Julian sighs dramatically. "I'm sensing judgment."

"Nah. Observation," I chuckle.

"You had kids before you got around to the ceremony." Fred claps his son on the back. "Bold strategy, son. Good thing she hasn't left you in the dust."

Julian lifts his glass again. "Marisol and I have always done things on our own time."

The laughter spreads around the table easily.

Irving turns his attention to me. The focus starts out subtle, but I brace for what's coming.

"So…" he says casually.

I know exactly where this is going.

"So," I repeat.

"You and Skylar."

My beer pauses halfway to my mouth. Julian glances between us.

I manage not to cough. "What about Sky?"

Irving nods at Julian. "You're telling me you and Marisol didn't notice?"

Fred raises an eyebrow.

Julian's eyebrows pinch together in confusion. "Notice what?"

Irving smiles slowly. "The change."

Great. I'm gonna have to kill him.

I take a sip of beer before asking, "What change?"

"Don't play. You and I both know why you flew her over here." Irving snorts.

Julian sets his glass down. "*Oh.*"

There it is. My turncoat friend. Irving's outed us before we're ready for the masses. I should be mad, but strangely I feel free. I run a hand through my hair.

"Things with me and Sky have…progressed," I admit.

Julian blinks once. "Progressed?"

"Yes."

Irving cheeses. "You dirty dog. You didn't confirm or deny."

"Huh." Julian chuckles quietly. "Took long enough. I wonder if Marisol knows."

"Fifteen years of tension is impressive." Irving nudges me.

I shrug. "Worth it. *She's* worth it."

Julian looks at me carefully. "You're serious."

"I've always been serious when it comes to Sky." The words come out before I filter them.

Four men stare at me. Waiting.

I smile despite myself. "She's *always* been it."

Fred shakes his head with a soft laugh. "Men of your generation waste a lot of time."

"You better not drag this out another decade." Irving points at me.

"I'm not rushing her," I protest.

"How in the hell would you be rushing her?" Julian asks.

"Because things changed on the way over and she asked me not to say anything," I try to explain. "Sky doesn't want to take the spotlight away from your wedding."

The four of them exchange looks.

Jose strokes his chin with his fingers. "Time is a funny thing. Sometimes you think you have plenty—"

"Sometimes you discover you don't," Fred finishes.

Irving lifts his glass again. "You've both already waited fifteen years."

Julian grins. "Clock's ticking."

I finish my beer and set down the empty glass. The advice isn't subtle.

But, it's solid.

In a few hours we'll be back at the castle for the rehearsal dinner.

Sky will be across from me again.

Publicly we're practicing patience.

Though, I'm starting to think it's overrated.

Chapter Thirteen

The Same Morning

THE SPA FILLS AN entire wing of the castle.

Underlit stone floors shimmer, walls are draped in tapestries of hushed forests. Tall, pointed-arch windows frame manicured rose gardens and morning light pools on the marble threshold of the reception area.

The gentle whisper of harp strings drifts from hidden speakers.

A flutter in my stomach reminds me why I'm late. It's been a whirlwind since Zach and I flew here on his private jet. Nearly every minute has been spent tangled in raw urgency. My nipples pebble at the thought of how many times he's made me come over the past forty-eight hours.

My heart swoons at the thought of a future together.

Our little secret until the wedding is over and we're able to come clean with our best friends. It'll be tough keeping this from Marisol.

"Skylar Morgan?" calls the receptionist with a perfect chignon, her practiced smile full of polite reproach.

My shoes squeak on polished stone as I approach. "Yes. Have they started without me?"

"No, they're finishing tea in the lounge." She beckons me down a carpeted hallway lined with oil paintings of falling water.

The lounge is a sanctuary of refined tranquility. Plush velvet armchairs in muted shades of pearl and blush are arranged in intimate clusters around low marble tables, their cool surfaces veined with delicate ribbons of gold. Crystal bowls overflow with freshly misted white roses, and sprigs of eucalyptus mingle subtly with the faintest hint of sandalwood.

Every detail in this castle speaks of understated luxury. From the gentle flicker of candlelight mirrored in the curved glass of antique lanterns to the soft weight of thick Persian rugs underfoot. It's a private haven where time slows and the world's noise is held at bay, leaving only comfort, beauty, and the gentle promise of renewal.

Marisol spots me the moment we step inside and lifts a dainty porcelain cup of chamomile. "There she is, Sky!"

From opposite ends of the sofa, Marisol and Julian's twin daughters, Sera and Soleil launch themselves at me. Soleil's cinnamon-scented curls brush my cheek; Sera squeezes me so snugly I practically taste her excitement.

"You're late," Soleil scolds, eyes shining.

Sera scoffs, "She's always late."

"I am not always late," I protest, hugging my goddaughters tightly.

"You almost missed Mom's birthday dinner last year," Soleil reminds me.

I brush the hair from her eyes. "New York City traffic."

"You flew here yesterday and this is the first time we've seen you," Sera counters.

I laugh, stepping back to admire their long, coltish legs and sun-bronzed skin. In the year since I've seen them, they've bloomed from chubby-cheeked girls into poised young tweens.

Marisol approaches, pulling me into a quick hug. Lupe, Marisol's mother, and Julian's mom, Véronique sit side by side, their silver spoons tapping porcelain teacups. Between them, Marisol's sister Miranda flips through a deck of nail-polish samples.

"Skylar," Véronique's French accent rolls off her tongue, "it's been too long."

"I know." I set my bag down on one of the chairs.

Lupe gestures at a tower piled with gorgeous pastries. "Eat something before you waste away."

"You don't want to miss these," Miranda holds up a chocolate croissant.

An attendant in crisp white arrives. "We're ready to begin treatments."

Like birds on a breeze, our group disperses into separate treatment rooms. Marisol and Miranda float down one corridor with Sera and Soleil. Lupe and Véronique follow another.

I change into a plush dove-gray robe and am led to a private suite filled with amber candles. For the next two hours I'm in a cocoon of bliss. Warm black sesame oil spreads along my spine as the therapist's hands knead every buried knot into oblivion. Next, a rose-and-cucumber mask cools my cheeks as gentle fingertips trace patterns across my forehead to free my mind from all stress.

When it ends, I drift to the manicure lounge where more velvet chairs are arranged across from each other in front of arched windows. At each station a steaming foot bath awaits dotted with rose petals. Marble tables display glossy bottles of polish in the same pale-rose shade and one glittering with translucent sparkles.

Sera and Soleil race to the sunlit chairs nearest the glass.

"I love the sparkles." Soleil holds up the bottle.

"What would a princess wedding be without sparkles?" Marisol surveys them and smiles. "We'll all get them so we match."

I manage to stifle my groan. I'm not a glitter girl, but I'll take one for the team.

Technicians in latex gloves trim our cuticles and shape nails at the same time our foot baths bubble.

Miranda leans back. "Princess wedding achieved?"

Marisol closes her eyes, face softening. "Finally."

Lupe laughs. "You've been planning this since childhood."

"That can't be true." Sera's eyes widen.

"Oh, there's a scrapbook," Miranda teases.

Marisol groans. "Miranda, is nothing sacred?"

We all drift into chatter about wedding dresses and heel heights.

Eventually, Miranda instigates gossip hour. "What's going on with Irving?"

Marisol snorts. "What's not going on with him?"

"C'mon. He broke up with Hudson, they'd been together for nearly a decade," Miranda says casually.

Lupe nods. "Good."

Véronique tilts her head. "Hudson was the tall one, right?"

"Yes." Marisol rolls her eyes. "Good riddance. He gave Irving an ultimatum. Move to London or break up."

"Irving's a big deal in Silicon Valley," I add softly. "Hudson was always trying to marginalize his accomplishments."

"Exactly," Marisol sighs. "He tried a power play and Irving finally had enough."

"Never works," Lupe declares.

Soleil wrinkles her nose "He was annoying."

"He was, and now he's gone." Marisol agrees.

"So... Let's talk about Zach." Miranda turns her gaze on me. I grip the armrest, willing indifference onto my face as I inadvertently replay how he made me come twice before I left this morning. "You probably know more about Zach than any of us."

Marisol catches my eye. "Zachary Bennett, the man who cannot be tamed."

Véronique tuts. "Is he still at it?"

"He'll be a bachelor forever." Marisol tilts her head. "If he's not careful."

"Why?" Sera asks.

"He can't seem to hold onto anything that matters," Marisol says flatly.

A technician dips her brush into pale-pink lacquer and sweeps it across my thumbnail smooth as silk. My pulse hammers.

Miranda adjusts to look at her sister. "He actually was involved with someone last year, though, wasn't he? I thought it was serious."

Marisol nods. "I never met her, her name was Lila, I think. Sky, do you have any intel?"

Suddenly, the lights are far too bright.

The technician lifts my hand and turns it gently under the light, examining the shape of my nails before dipping the brush back into a bottle of polish for the second coat. I watch the motion without really seeing it, the smooth stroke of color across my nail suddenly the only thing holding my focus.

Lila?

The name echoes in my mind like a dropped glass.

I blink once, then again, forcing my shoulders to settle back into the cushioned chair as if nothing inside me has shifted.

Because everything absolutely has.

Even before recent events, Zach and I have talked about everything happening in our lives for years. Flights across time zones. Business transactions. Our dating foibles. Hopes. Dreams. Stories about childhood or whatever book one of us was reading.

Everything.

Or at least I believed it was everything.

My voice seems distant when it finally comes out. "He never mentioned anyone named Lila to me."

The words land casual enough no one notices I'm about to throw up my breakfast.

"So?" Véronique tilts her head slightly from the chair beside Lupe. "What happened, Marisol?"

Marisol lifts one shoulder as the technician begins painting her nails. "He let it fade. Told Julian he was too busy for a relationship."

"Work as an excuse." Lupe's eyebrow rises slowly.

Marisol nods, the corner of her mouth turning down. "Always work."

I stare down at my hands as the polish dries. Why didn't he tell me?

Why didn't she?

Two hours ago I woke wrapped in his arms and he told me this wasn't a fling. He promised things dangerously close to forever.

My chest seizes.

Did he use the same lines on her?

Soleil swings her legs in the pedicure chair and wrinkles her nose. "Uncle Zach is ridiculous."

"Yeah. If you love someone," Sera nods with complete certainty, "you keep them."

The simplicity resonates more deeply than anything the adults have said.

Tears burn under my eyes. I want to believe in Zach.

Choosing me.

Choosing us.

Yet suddenly a shadow sits in the story I thought I knew.

A relationship he never mentioned with a woman with whose name I've never heard.

For the first time since waking beside him, a quiet doubt takes hold.

How much of Zach's life do I truly know?

And how much have I only assumed he was telling me?

Chapter Fourteen

ZACHARY

A Few Hours Later

THE REHEARSAL IS CHAOS from the first minute.

Castles look romantic in photographs. In reality they're stone labyrinths designed centuries before anyone imagined modern events with seating charts, a room full of control freaks, and two twelve-year-old twins who refuse to walk down an aisle without spinning.

By the time the wedding planner claps her hands for the third time and asks everyone to start over, half the wedding party is laughing and the other half is trying to remember where they're supposed to stand.

I should be enjoying this. Instead, my attention keeps drifting to the same place.

Skylar.

She's halfway down the aisle with Sera and Soleil, crouched slightly so she can straighten Soleil's sash while whispering something to make both girls giggle. The candlelight from the chapel sconces catches the violet streak in her hair and throws soft gold across her cheekbones.

She looks calm. Focused.

Beautiful in a way making it difficult to notice anyone else. Which is inconvenient because this room is full of people who know us very well.

The pub crawl ended hours ago. Julian insisted we head back early enough to appear respectable for the rehearsal, which meant a long walk through Old Town with the five of us pretending the afternoon hadn't included more beer than was strictly necessary.

Even with a delightful day spent with my closest guy friends, my mind kept drifting back to the castle.

I missed Sky. I couldn't stop daydreaming about making love to her this morning. Wondering if we could slip in some time together before dinner.

I told myself I was being ridiculous. We'll have all night. Tomorrow, after the wedding, all bets are off. Hell. If I have my say, she and I will have the rest of our lives.

Anyway, apparently two hours apart was enough to make me lose my mind.

When we got back to the castle I tried her door. Locked. I sent a text. No response.

I figured she was busy with Marisol. Told myself it meant nothing. Then rehearsal started and she's barely looked at me. Every time we get close, she finds a reason to turn away. A flower adjustment. A quiet word with Marisol. A hand on one of the girls' shoulders guiding them back into place.

At first I thought I was imagining it.

Until it was clear I wasn't.

Sky and I are paired for the ceremony. From my place near the front, I watch her practice walking up the aisle carrying a bouquet placeholder. The second we're close enough to touch, her face freezes in cool composure.

I'm standing near the altar, awkwardly pretending to listen while the planner explains once again where the bridal party should stand. The next hour is a whole lot of walk here. Pause here. Turn toward the officiant here. Our hands brush once when the planner repositions us and Sky pulls hers back as if she's touched a hot stove.

No smile. No secret glances. None of the heat lingers from the countless times I've been inside her over the past forty-eight hours.

Only distance.

By the sixth practice run, everyone is over it. Sera twirls instead of walking. Soleil sings a Taylor Swift song. Marisol sighs and Julian eyes roll so overtly, we all stifle laughs.

Sky remains calm and focused and gently guides both girls back into place.

"Walk," the planner points.

"We *are* walking," Soleil insists.

Marisol throws her hands up. "You're dancing."

Everyone breaks into laughter again. Sky finally glances up and, for a second, our eyes meet. Barely long enough to register before she turns back to the girls.

My stomach roils. Nope. I'm not imagining it. Something is way off.

Finally, the planner declares the rehearsal "good enough," allowing us to dissolve into casual conversation. The procession toward the dining room happens in loose waves. Family first, then the bridal party.

Sky is immediately swallowed by the girls. Soleil hooks an arm through hers. Sera takes her other side. They draw her over to Marisol and Lupe, where they form one seamless little cluster of bright voices, dark curls, and wedding energy.

I don't get within ten feet of her.

Dinner takes place in a smaller hall tonight. Lower ceilings. Dark wood paneling. The windows overlook the gardens where dusk is settling over the hedges and stone paths. The table glows in candlelight. White linen. Gold-rimmed glasses. Small arrangements of pale roses and greenery. Plates of fresh bread and whipped butter already wait at intervals along the center.

By the time I enter, Sky is already seated between Soleil and Marisol on one side, with Sera beside Miranda a few seats down. I end up directly across from her because fate, apparently, enjoys irony.

Voices overlap in every direction. Julian and his father are debating the proper order of toasts. Véronique compliments the flowers. Irving is on his second glass of wine looking entirely too pleased with himself.

Sky still won't look at me.

Her attention is fixed on the twins as they chatter about tomorrow's flower petals and whether they are allowed to eat cake before the adults. She smiles. Nods. Tears bread into neat pieces and passes the basket to Miranda.

Sky's freezing me out.

I clear my throat softly and reach for my water. Nothing. Not even a flicker.

The first course arrives. A clear consommé with herbs and delicate, tiny dumplings floating in the center. Sky lifts her spoon. Blows once. Tastes it.

I know the exact shape of her mouth when she's pleased by something because I've spent fifteen years cataloging things I never admitted mattered.

By the second course, conversation and wine is flowing over roast chicken with root vegetables and a rich mushroom sauce. Fred tells a story about Julian at fourteen trying to impress his high school girlfriend with a borrowed guitar and exactly three chords. Laughter ensues.

Sky laughs. I catch the curve of her smile. A sharp pull of relief hits me square in the center and makes me stupid enough to think I can fix what's wrong with one well-timed glance.

I address her directly. "Sky."

She hears me. I know she does because her shoulders slope almost imperceptibly. No acknowledgement though.

"So," Miranda reaches for her wine, "how was the famous Prague pub crawl bachelor party?"

"Uneventful," Irving deadpans.

Fred snorts into his glass.

Jose smiles. "You mean irresponsible."

"Only in the best possible way." I raise my glass and once again try to catch Sky's eye.

Nothing.

Julian laughs. "Hudson would have hated every minute."

Irving sets his glass down with more force than necessary. "Hudson hated most things I enjoyed."

I glance at Sky's face, lightness drains from her expression.

Lupe lifts a brow. "Good riddance. He wasn't a good fit."

"He was a fraud." Irving emits a short laugh with no amusement in it.

All of us freeze. Julian even stops cutting his chicken.

"The man spent ten years pretending we were partners." Irving shrugs one shoulder, but there's an edge under the movement. "What he really wanted was an accessory. Someone to orbit his life while calling it love."

No one interrupts him.

"He loved the optics," Irving continues, voice calm in a way anger often is when it's old. "The right dinners. The right cities. The right photos. But any time I wanted something for myself, there was suddenly a problem. Silicon Valley was provincial. You guys were distractions. My work mattered less than his because his sounded grander over cocktails."

Marisol mutters, "Asshole."

"Exactly." Irving reaches for his wine but doesn't drink it yet. "I wasted too much time thinking effort would turn him into someone honest."

Something goes very still inside me. Across from me, Sky finally makes direct eye contact and she's not giving sympathy for Irving. Or abstract disapproval for Hudson.

It's disgust. Aimed squarely at me.

Nothing loud or dramatic. No one else would notice the brief, unmistakable clench around her mouth. Or the flicker in her eyes I've often seen when she speaks about the opposing party in cases she tries.

It's a look that has never directed at *me*.

I stop breathing for half a second. Something shifted between breakfast and now. Whatever it is, it's clear I've disappointed her somehow.

The rest of the conversation resumes in fragments. Someone changes the subject to tomorrow's weather. Julian asks Fred about the timing of the cars. Miranda starts teasing the twins again.

I hear almost none of it.

All I can see is the way Sky interacts with everyone except me.

What the hell happened?

Chapter Fifteen

Two Hours Later

DINNER DRAGS ON LONGER than I ever imagined.

Julian is halfway through another explanation about the timing of tomorrow's events, gesturing wildly while Fred listens with exaggerated patience. Miranda laughs softly at something Marisol whispers to her, and Lupe discusses flowers with Véronique as if their arrangement holds the fate of the ceremony.

Plates were cleared over an hour ago. Candles burn low while wine continues to appear as if the staff senses no one is quite ready to leave. From the outside looking in, the evening looks perfect. Warm light, soft laughter, the easy rhythm of old friends sharing a long meal.

I'm playing my part. Smiling when someone looks my way. Lifting my glass when appropriate. Chatting with everyone around me. Yet, inside, my chest is equally compressed and hollow all at once.

Servers move quietly between chairs, gathering the last of the dishes. Someone mentions tomorrow's weather. Another toast rises somewhere near the end of the table.

Exhausted from keeping up appearances, I fix my eyes on my wine glass.

Across from me, I can sense Zach watching. If I meet his gaze, the fragile composure holding me together might shatter before we leave.

Her name keeps echoing in my mind.

Lila.

It shouldn't matter. People date. People fuck. For most of my adult life Zach and I did both with other people. We were simply friends who knew each other too well to complicate things. At least that's the story I've told myself whenever the thought drifted too close to the truth.

Except we weren't.

We were always something complicated and electric and unfinished. Something neither of us dared to name because naming it meant risking everything else.

Now we've crossed the line in the most spectacular way possible. I keep hearing Marisol's voice again.

He can't seem to hold onto anything that matters.

I twist the stem of my wine glass between my fingers and focus on breathing slowly. Maybe I misunderstood. Maybe it meant nothing.

Maybe—

No.

The worst part is he didn't tell me.

I thought he trusted me with his secrets. Now I'm wondering if I mistook honesty for comfort. Especially if there were corners of his life I never knew existed.

"Sky?"

Marisol's voice pulls me back into the present. I blink and realize everyone is standing. Dinner is finally over.

Chairs scrape softly across the floor as we begin drifting out the doors in clusters. Julian wraps an arm around Marisol's shoulders and kisses her temple. The girls are already halfway to the hallway arguing about whose turn it is to brush their teeth first.

I rise carefully, smoothing my dress down with deliberate movements.

Don't look at him.

Don't look at him.

Don't—too late.

Zach pushes his chair back. His eyes find mine immediately. Concern flashes across his face.

I look away.

"Goodnight, everyone." I force a smile. "Big day tomorrow."

A chorus of agreements follows.

As everyone hugs and kisses goodnight, I slip into the hallway, hoping I'm quick enough to avoid Zach.

The corridor outside the dining hall is quieter. Stone floors. Soft lantern light. The low murmur of distant voices fading behind me as I move deeper into the castle. My heels click on the stone as I head for the staircase leading to the guest rooms. I'm nearly there. If I can get to my room before Zach catches up—

"*Sky.*"

His footsteps close the distance behind me quickly, long strides eating the hallway. I reach my door and fumble with the key just as his hand lands beside my shoulder.

"*Skylar.*"

I close my eyes. "Please don't."

"Don't what?" His breath warms my neck.

"Don't push me right now." My voice sounds steadier than I feel. "Tomorrow is Marisol's wedding. I don't want to ruin her day."

His silence stretches behind me, but he doesn't move. Then he finally says, "Clearly, something is wrong."

I turn slowly to face him. Up close his expression is impossible to ignore.

Concern. Confusion. A trace of hurt.

"Yes, but we can talk later." I flick my eyes away.

"Sky." This time, the way he says my name makes something in my chest twist painfully. "We're best friends first. If something is bothering you, I need to know."

The gentleness in his voice makes my resolve wobble. I shake my head once. "Please don't push."

"Shutting me out hurts worse than anything you might say." He doesn't move. Or step back.

I close my eyes briefly. When I open them again, I push the door to my room wider and step inside.

"Fine."

He follows me inside. Candlelight from the bedside lamp glows softly across the bed where we spent last night tangled together. The memory of it flashes through my mind with cruel clarity.

I turn to face him. "Who the fuck is Lila?"

Her name thuds like a stone. For a second he simply stares at me. Then he starts laughing.

Not a quiet chuckle. A full, startled chortle.

"You think this is *funny*?" My voice cracks despite my effort to keep it steady.

His laughter dies instantly. "No...Sky—"

"Marisol said you were seeing someone last year," I continue, words rushing out now. "Someone serious. Someone you liked so much she and Julian thought you might finally settle down."

He stares at me, stunned.

"You never mentioned her to *me*," I finish quietly. "Why?"

Silence. Then he exhales slowly and rubs a hand through his hair. "Oh. My, God."

"What?"

His eyes meet mine again. "Lila isn't a woman."

"What?" My heart stutters.

"She's my assistant's dog."

My brain struggles to process the sentence. "A dog."

"Yes."

"A *dog*."

"Yes."

Tears spill before I can stop them.

Zach steps forward immediately. "Hey—"

"I thought..." My voice breaks. "I thought you kept something important from me on purpose. To hide it."

His face softens instantly. "No. Never. I made her up."

"What?" I'm so confused I don't know what to think.

"Julian and Marisol have been riding me for years about you," he says quietly. "About how I let the best thing in my life sit right in front of me without doing anything about it."

My breath catches.

"So I invented a girlfriend." He rubs his forehead.

I throw up my hands. "And named her after your assistant's dog?"

"In my defense," he says carefully, "Lila was in the office. Seemed easy enough."

A shaky laugh escapes me through the tears. Relief floods through my chest so fast it almost makes me dizzy.

"Hey." Zach pulls me into his arms.

"I'm sorry," I whisper.

"You actually thought I was hiding someone." He pets the back of my head.

I clutch his shoulder. "I thought you lied to me."

"Sky." His arms knot around me. "If you want to know the truth, ask."

I pull back enough to look at him and nearly start crying again. "You could have told me."

"How about I tell you this: I've been in love with you for years." Zach thumbs my jaw.

"You could have told me."

"Yeah, so could you."

Fair point.

My fingers curl into his shirt. "So what happens now?"

He kisses the tip of my nose.

"We finally stop pretending."

Chapter Sixteen

Later That Evening

Sky is breathtaking.

The sharp edge of hurt has softened, leaving something open and uncertain behind it.

Vulnerability. Hope. The same mix I emotions I'm wrestling with.

I move closer. "Sky."

Her eyes lift to mine.

The kiss begins slowly, almost cautious at first. Not the frantic heat from the past couple days. Something deeper, steadier. My mouth brushes hers once, then again, until she angles into it and tension melts into warmth.

Her hands slide up my arms as she kisses me back. The familiarity of it sends a quiet pulse of relief through me.

I pull back just enough to see her face again. "I meant what I said about loving you."

For a second she studies me as if weighing the words and testing whether she believes them. After all, we spent years feigning none of this existed.

"I love you too."

Her words settle between us like something long over-due finally finding its place. For a moment neither of us moves. I watch her face soften after saying it, the tension in her shoulders easing as if the truth itself carries weight she's been holding for years.

My hand finds hers. Her fingers slip easily into mine, warm and familiar, and I lift them to my lips for a brief kiss before standing.

"Come here," I whisper.

She lets me lead her the few steps to the velvet couch near the window. The fabric is deep green and catches the candlelight as she sits, the glow tracing the curve of her hair and the gentle rise and fall of her breathing.

Instead of sitting beside her, I lower myself slowly to my knees in front of her.

The movement surprises her. "Zach—"

"Let me." I scan her face for approval.

From here I can see every flicker of emotion crossing her face. The softness in her eyes. The way her fingers coil against the cushion beside her.

"I spent fifteen years pretending I could live without this," my hands settle lightly at her waist, "without you."

Her breath trembles and she looks down at our hands for a moment, gathering herself.

"I should have asked you about Lila, instead of letting my mind run wild." Her thumb traces slowly along my knuckles before she lifts her eyes again. "I don't want to fall into the patterns my parents had. Assuming the worst. Letting silence grow into something ugly."

My fingers close more firmly around hers. "You won't. Not with me. You can trust this."

"You don't have to prove anything." She studies my face as if searching for any hesitation.

"We've known each other too long to start doubting now." I bring her hand to my lips and kiss her knuckles one by one. "Yes, everything changed between us in the past few days, but our foundation didn't disappear. If anything, it's stronger. We know each other better than anyone."

Her gaze softens.

"We can trust each other." I nudge forward just enough to slowly sweep my lips along hers.

Her laugh is soft and shaky. When I pull back, my hands slide gently along her sides, holding her there. This moment deserves patience.

I'm in no hurry at all.

I take my time, savoring the sight of her as I pull the dress over her head. She's left in nothing but her lace panties, breasts exposed, nipples hardening under my gaze. I edge in, trailing kisses down her collarbone. Her pulse quickens beneath my touch.

"You're so beautiful," I whisper, as my fingers trace over her dusky nipples. I take one into my mouth, swirling my tongue around the sensitive peak. She gasps, tangling her fingers in my hair, urging me closer.

I move lower, kissing my way down her stomach, savoring the way her body responds to my touch. I hook my fingers into the waistband of her panties and sweep them down her legs, exposing her fully to me. She's breathtaking. Her pussy glistens with arousal, and I can hardly contain the need building inside me.

"I want to taste you." My voice is thick with desire as I kneel before her.

Skimming my lips along her inner thigh, I inhale her scent. She's trembling, anticipation thrumming through her as I inch closer to her core.

With a determination, I trace my tongue along her folds, tasting her sweetness as I plunge into her. Her back bows when I tease her clit with small flicks of my tongue. I watch her face and the way her eyes flutter shut, lips parting as soft moans escape.

It's the most beautiful sight I've ever seen.

"God, your taste is addicting," I swirl my tongue through her sweet nectar.

I'm mesmerized by the way her body responds, her hips bucking against my devouring mouth.

"Zach, please," she pleads, and it drives me wild. I want to hear her beg for me and unravel completely. "I'm so close."

"Come for me, baby," I urge, my fingers moving faster, mouth working her clit. "I love you."

Her walls clench around my fingers and she cries out when her orgasm crashes over her in waves. I don't stop, my mouth and fingers work together to prolong her pleasure.

"Again." I lick her entire slit, spreading her lips so I don't miss anything.

I want to see Sky lose herself completely and shatter around me. I lift her legs over my shoulders, allowing the heat of her pussy to engulf my mouth as I devour her. When she comes again, her loud, staccato cries fill the room.

When I finally pull back, my chest heaves as I look into her eyes. Her face is flushed and radiant, the aftermath of her pleasure painting her with a glow making me want to give her more.

I lift her onto my lap, guiding her down onto my cock. The hot, wet sensation is overwhelming and I can't help but groan when I fill her completely. Positioning her just right, I hold her in place, making sure her clit brushes my pubic bone. I thrust into her. The angle is perfect, my cock hits her G-spot with every movement and her body responds to the dual stimulation by frantically moving in rhythm with mine.

"God, you feel incredible." My voice is heavy is with pleasure.

My hands span her ass to guide her movements, until the sound of our moans and skin slapping together is all I can hear. She's dripping with arousal. Her body writhes with mine.

"Zach, oh God, *Zach*." Sky's nails dig into my shoulders as she rides me harder.

The tension builds between us, a sweet ache threatening to pull us both under. She constricts around me again and I know she's close. "Yeah. Squeeze my cock. Take what you need."

With a final cry, she tumbles over the edge, her body seizing as she comes. It takes every ounce of self-control not to follow her into bliss, but I want this moment to last as long as possible.

I lift her off me, her body limp and sated as I carry her to the bed. Laying her down carefully, I position myself behind her to achieve my own release. The sight of her ass high in the air and her glistening pussy drives me insane. I slide into her tight heat all the way to my root.

The angle is perfect, allowing me to hit her g-spot with every thrust. Gripping her hips, I guide her pussy back and forth on my cock. Immediately, her body responds to mine and I can feel the tension building again.

I reach around with my fingers to find her clit, circling it in time with my rapid thrusts. I drive us both higher and higher and we're unable to contain the feral sounds of pleasure which echo off the stone walls.

"Zach, I *can't*—" Her words are cut off by a shriek when she comes again.

The sensation is too much. I can't hold back any longer. I fill her to the brim, the pleasure so intense it leaves me breathless.

Afterward, I pull out of her to glimpse my come seeping out of her pussy and dripping down her thigh. It's a primal, possessive sight.

Sky's mine, and I want everyone to know it.

I collapse onto the bed beside her and cuddle her close as we both struggle to catch our breath. We lie there entwined, the warmth of our intimacy lingering.

She turns to face me, her eyes soft and content. "Zach, I'm a little mad we've wasted so many years *not* fucking. Together, we're incredible."

"We are." My heart swells with love and happiness. "In the spirit of being truthful, there's something else I need to tell you before you hear it from Julian."

Her eyes search mine, amusement urges me on. "Oh God. What is it now? Another fake girlfriend with a dog?"

"No." My fingers comb once through my hair before clasping her hand. "I sold the company."

Her brows lift a touch.

"It's why I disappeared before the wedding. I was with Julian to complete the paperwork." Her fingers close around mine, listening. "I planned on telling you this weekend, but…"

Sky looks at me expectantly.

"I wanted to take my shot first." My thumb brushes across her knuckles where our hands rest on my chest. "One thing isn't negotiable." I hold her gaze. "I'm not letting you walk away from me again, Sky."

She studies me for a long moment. "Don't worry. You're not getting rid of me, Zach Bennett."

Relief loosens something deep in my chest.

I knot my arms around her and stare into the dark.

The promise of our future settles quietly between us.

Wedding or not, tomorrow we stop hiding.

Chapter Seventeen

The Next Day

EARLY AFTERNOON LIGHT POURS into Marisol's suite in long ribbons of gold.

Her room occupies the corner of the castle's east wing, a sprawling space meant for royalty and, apparently, now repurposed for bridal chaos. Two walls of floor-to-ceiling windows overlook the gardens below, where hedges form careful geometric patterns and a gravel path winds to the chapel.

The glam squad arrived an hour ago and have transformed the sitting room into a command center. Curling irons warm on marble trays. Makeup palettes lie open like tiny artist studios. Racks of dresses stand along one wall, silk and chiffon catching the light whenever someone passes.

Marisol sits in the center of it all.

Her robe is ivory silk embroidered with small flowers along the collar. A hairstylist works a curling wand through her dark hair while another kneels beside her with a tray of pearl hairpins arranged in careful rows.

Over by the wardrobe, her wedding gown hangs alone on its rack.

The dress is pure fantasy. Ivory silk fitted through the bodice before exploding into layers of floating tulle. Hand-stitched blush and pale-blue flowers trail along the train, catching the light each time the fabric moves. A seamstress stands nearby, steaming the skirt with the care usually reserved for museum pieces.

Or, a Disney princess wedding.

Marisol always said if she waited long enough to marry Julian Monroe, she was going to do it properly. Seventeen years apparently qualifies as long enough.

The rest of us orbit around her. The supporting cast in a particularly glamorous production.

Miranda inclines against the window, sipping coffee while scrolling through her phone. Lupe sits in a make-up chair nearby while a stylist blends soft color along her cheekbones. Véronique studies her blue gown in the full-length mirror.

Sera and Soleil claimed the velvet sofa near the balcony doors. It's a throne built for two. The girls watch themselves in the mirror propped on the wall as a stylist stands behind them weaving their dark curls into intricate braided crowns.

"This is the best day of my life." Soleil is practically vibrating with excitement.

Sera rolls her eyes. "It's Mom and Dad's wedding."

"It's our wedding too," Soleil declares with absolute certainty.

Marisol laughs, barely turning in her chair. "You're not wrong, my sweet girl. I've been planning this since before you were born. Now we'll all finally get to experience it."

The stylist lifts a small dish of glittering pins. "More sparkles?"

"Yes," the twins answer in perfect unison.

I glance over from the window with mock surrender. "*Elegant* sparkles."

The girls beam like royalty as the first glinting pin disappears into Soleil's braid.

I sit beside them while someone finishes spritzing the soft waves in my hair. My freshly-steamed dress hangs beside the twins', a blush-colored gown with a flowing skirt and matching ballet flats.

Pausing for a moment, I simply take it in. Everything carries a quiet kind of joy. Laughter rises and falls around me, familiar voices weaving together.

Gratitude settles quietly in my chest.

Life doesn't often slow down enough for all of us to be in the same place at the same time. Work, cities, flights and responsibilities scatter everyone in different directions. Gatherings with all five of us are rare.

Yet here we are. My oldest friends. Their families. The twins who have grown up so fast they're suddenly old enough to stand beside their mother on her wedding day.

Marisol and Julian have taken an unconventional path to get here. Seventeen years of love, arguments, children, and life before finally deciding to throw the wedding they always joked about. We're joyfully witnessing a love story we all helped write.

I'm proud to be here for this moment and the chance to stand beside my best friend while she finally gets her princess day.

Not to mention the unexpected gift the past few days have given me.

Zach lingers in the back of my mind. A warm secret I'm dying to reveal.

God, the way he looked at me last night. Like I matter to him more than anything else. For the first time in a long while, the future isn't rushing toward me faster than I can comprehend.

Now I'm in control. Opening an entire new chapter.

Choice.

The memory of last night lingers under my skin. Zach's hands all over me. His voice and the certainty in his eyes when he told me he wasn't letting me walk away again.

A smile slips onto my face before I can stop it.

I'm standing near the tall mirror while the stylist secures the last pin in my hair, soft curls falling over my shoulders. In the reflection, Marisol catches my eyes.

She doesn't say anything.

She just gives me a look.

The look.

The one she perfected at twenty-two sitting in the back row of Contracts pretending to understand cold calls.

I glance away and smooth the skirt of my dress.

Around us the suite buzzes with last-minute movement. Miranda helps the twins into their shoes while Lupe adjusts a bracelet on Véronique's wrist. One stylist gathers brushes from the long table while another folds garment bags.

"Alright." Miranda claps once. "Let's move before someone changes their mind."

The twins rush out the door and disappear into the hallway. Lupe and Véronique follow behind them, talking quietly as they go. Miranda isn't far behind.

I'm halfway to the door when Marisol's hand closes gently around my wrist. "Hold on." She studies my face for a moment. "You look different."

"Good different?" I tilt my head.

Her eyebrows lift marginally. "Yeah."

"Something happened." I lower my voice as we pause beside the doorway. "We can talk about it after the wedding."

"Spill." Marisol folds her arms, studying me.

I smooth the front of my dress, trying to find the words.

"It's Zach, right?" She fixes me with a pointed stare.

I exhale, resigned, and glance down the hallway to make sure the others are still waiting near the elevator. "That obvious?"

"Duh." Marisol nods slowly.

"Fine. We slept together." I lower my voice even further. "On the plane. And…pretty much every chance we've had since."

Hearing the words out loud is strange and wonderful all at once.

Marisol's reaction isn't shock. Her mouth curves into a satisfied smile as she lets out a quiet breath. "Why didn't you tell me?"

"I didn't want to spoil your day." I shake my head, laughing softly.

"Spoil. Schmoil. Fifteen years plus seventy-two hours," a grin tugs at her lips. "Thank God you two finally stopped wasting time."

"He's…incredible." Heat creeps up my neck and I look down, twisting the dainty bracelet encircling my wrist.

Her face softens immediately. "I'm really happy for you."

"It feels fast," I admit, glancing out the window where the garden ceremony chairs wait in perfect rows. "Also slow."

"No, overdue." Marisol reaches out and squeezes my hand.

I swallow. "I'm so fucking scared."

"Sky." She steps closer, her hand still wrapped around mine. "Zach has loved you for *years*."

I shake my head subtly. "He told you?"

"He didn't have to." Her thumb strokes lightly against my knuckles before she releases my hand. "I'm glad you two finally stopped pretending."

Voices echo down the hallway as the others gather near the elevator. The twins' laughter carries from around the corner. Marisol glances over, then back at me before stepping away.

"Come on." She gestures at the noise. "Right now, your job is to walk beside me and look happy."

"Easiest job in the world. What about the rest?" I ask, following her down the corridor.

She smiles as the elevator doors slide open.

"The rest will sort itself out."

Chapter Eighteen

A Couple Hours Later

I SHOULD BE FOCUSED on my duties as best man.

Instead I'm thinking about Sky because I'm a lovesick fool.

The groom's quarters are in the chapel building on the castle grounds, tall windows frame Prague's red tile roofs and pale church towers rising from a distance beyond the gardens.

Inside, the space gives half royal dressing chamber, half old-world study. Dark walnut wardrobes, brocade chairs gathered near the windows, and a long oak table cluttered with cufflinks, watches, and half-empty whiskey glasses. Polished shoes line the wall beneath the wardrobe while the midnight-blue tux jackets hang in a careful row.

Disney princes.

Marisol committed to the bit down to the very last detail.

Truthfully, our tuxes are classic. Satin lapels in deep ink blue instead of black. Crisp white shirts with covered buttons. Silk bow ties. Gold cufflinks shaped like little crowns. Even the pocket squares are embroidered with a custom crest, which somehow makes the whole thing more ridiculous and perfect.

Julian stands in front of the mirror fastening his tie with fixed concentration. Fred sits near the window in one armchair, Jose in the other, each holding a low glass of whiskey and looking entirely too relaxed for fathers on wedding day duty. Irving drapes himself across the back of a velvet settee with all the grace of a man born to be inappropriate in historic buildings.

The last seventy-two hours have wrecked me in the best possible way. The plane. Sky's room. The look on her face last night when she finally believed I'm all in. The way she said she loved me like the words scared her and steadied her all at once.

Best of all, how she felt in my arms after. Soft, pliant ,and present. Our future has suddenly developed a pulse.

I haven't had nearly enough sleep. Also: I do not care.

Julian gives up on the bow tie and looks at me in the mirror. "You're somewhere else."

"Nah, man. I'm right here.," I adjust one cuff.

Irving twirls a finger around his head. "Physically yes. Mentally...not so much."

Julian turns from the mirror, studying me now with the same skeptic sneer he used in law school when he knew I was lying but wanted to watch me do it anyway. "Didn't sleep well?"

"I slept fine." I feign nonchalance.

"Well, I didn't sleep last night." Irving points his glass at me like he's about to submit evidence. "My suite shares a wall with Sky's."

Fred's brows go up. Julian stills.

I glare.

Irving takes his time, savoring his moment before he continues. "Care to give us an update, Romeo?"

I stare at him. He stares back.

Julian's mouth parts. "Wait. More progression?"

"Mm-hmm." Irving nods at me without looking away.

Julian points at me with one hand and at Irving with the other as if physically connecting the dots in the air. "You dirty dog."

"Walls are old. Very little mystery survives in this castle." Irving lifts one shoulder.

I rub a hand over the back of my neck and look to the ceiling for half a second, mostly because not smiling is impossible.

"Zach." Julian walks closer, his expression somewhere between triumph and disbelief.

No point pretending. "We're in love."

All the men go still. As if a long-running theory has just become fact.

Irving tips his head. "So, counselor, you want to tell the class what your intentions are?"

"I'm gonna lock her down." I look down while fastening my second cufflink, buying myself a second.

Julian gives a disbelieving laugh. "What the fuck?"

"And then." Irving points at me again.

"And then," I'm unable to stop my grin now, "we'll all gather for our wedding someday soon."

Julian folds his arms and studies me for a long moment. "Hold up, now. This is you. Please don't fuck around with her feelings."

The question lands cleanly. I lift my gaze.

Irving watches me closely now, all humor drained from his face.

"I alluded to this yesterday and it's taken me nearly two decades to admit it, but Sky is and always has been the love of my life." The truth of it settles so naturally it surprises me. "She feels the same way and we've both been stupid idiots who have wasted far too much time."

Silence.

Julian shakes his head as if he's been personally inconvenienced by my late arrival to common sense. "Thank Christ. Marisol and I have listened to both of you pine in different ways for years."

"Took long enough." Irving lifts his glass.

Julian points straight at my chest. "Put a ring on it."

"Intend to." I huff out a laugh.

"Sooner rather than later," Julian instructs.

I glance down at the crown cufflink glinting at my wrist and think of Sky. From all the years we've deepened our friendship to how she looked in bed last night after crying over a fake girlfriend named after a dog.

Julian notices the shift in me. "What's going on, Zach?"

I drag a breath through my chest and answer without planning to. "I can't believe I'm selling my company."

Four heads turn.

Irving straightens first. "What's next?"

I look at my friends, at the fathers, at the ridiculous prince tux hanging off my shoulders, and think about how little I care about titles compared to the woman in the chapel waiting downstairs.

"Sky," I answer. "Whatever happens, Sky is the focus."

A knock sounds at the door before anyone can keep going. The wedding planner slips her head inside, headset on, clipboard in hand. "Gentlemen. Guests are seated."

Julian's face changes in an instant. The jokes vanish. The groom face reappears.

Fred rises first and claps him on the shoulder. Jose follows with a quiet, firm hug. Irving straightens his jacket and drains the last of his drink. I pick up my own glass from the mantel and set it aside untouched.

No more delays.

We leave the suite together and move through the corridor. Footsteps echo distinctly on the stone. Somewhere below, music drifts upward through the stairwell, strings only, sweet and bright and delicately unreal.

The chapel doors stand open. Candlelight washes the pale stone walls. Flowers climb the ends of the pews in white, blush, and the faintest blue, tying the whole princess fantasy together without tipping into absurdity. Sunlight still lingers through the stained glass high above, painting the aisle with scattered color.

I take my place beside Irving and look up once. The doors at the back of the chapel open and the ceremony begins.

Sixty people rise as one.

Immediately, I locate Sky, who stands near Marisol. Her blush dress falls in soft lines to her ankles and her hair is pinned back so her curls spill over one shoulder. She stepped out of the same fairytale as the rest of this castle.

Her eyes find mine for a second. Then the music changes.

Sera and Soleil go first, their pale-blue dresses float around them as they scatter flower petals. Miranda and Sky follow, radiant in silver-blue. Then Lupe and Véronique, elegant and proud and trying not to cry before the bride even appears.

When Marisol steps into the doorway the entire room draws breath. Her gown glows. There's no other word for it. Ivory silk fitted close through the bodice, then opening into layers of tulle and hand-stitched flowers trailing behind her in a soft cloud of pale color.

Julian forgets how to stand for a moment. She walks toward him slowly, her face lit with happiness. Julian takes her hands the second she reaches him.

"Most couples stand here to promise a life together." The officiant smiles as if she's been waiting for this too, her voice carrying easily through the chapel. "Julian and Marisol are doing this on their own terms."

Laughter ripples gently throughout the chapel.

The officiant continues. "They have lived through youth, career, parenthood, grief, joy, reinvention, and ordinary Tuesdays. They have chosen each other for seventeen years. Today they are not beginning love. They are honoring it."

Julian goes first with his vows, gazing at Marisol like he's still astonished she made it all the way here with him. "We grew up together. Not in a straight line. Not neatly. We did everything backward and somehow still ended up exactly where we belonged."

Marisol's eyes glisten.

He squeezes her hands. "I promise to keep choosing you. On good days. On terrible days. When life is easy and when it makes no sense at all. I promise to be your home even when the map changes."

A few people in the pews openly cry at this point.

"Most princess stories end at the wedding." Marisol smiles through tears when she begins her own vows. "Ours started long before it. We built a family before we built a ceremony. We learned patience before we learned timing. We had children before we had matching rings." She laughs, her eyes fixed on Julian. "I promise the same thing I've promised you in a thousand ordinary ways for seventeen years. My loyalty. My honesty. My joy. My hand in yours through every version of our life."

The vows strike a chord because Sky and I did it in reverse too. Friendship before confession. History before courage. Years before touch.

By the time the rings slide into place and the officiant pronounces them married, the chapel fills with the quiet force of everyone who helped carry them here. Years of friendship, family, and stubborn devotion infuse them with blessings.

Applause breaks out. Sera and Soleil practically vibrate with triumph. Julian kisses Marisol, dipping her low.

While everyone else rises and turns and reaches for tissues, I look across the front of the chapel.

Sky is already looking at me.

Everything around us blurs.

The flowers. The candles. The music.

None of it matters as much as the quiet certainty in her face.

Whatever comes next, we're doing it together from now on.

Chapter Nineteen

Later That Night

THE RECEPTION HALL HAS been utterly transformed.

Earlier it held the long banquet tables filled with dinner conversation and delicious food. Now the space comes alive in a different way.

Staff have discreetly cleared the dining area for dancing, pushing the linen-covered tables back against the stone walls where candles flicker beside tall arrangements of blush roses and pale-blue hydrangeas. Small strings of lights wind through the wooden beams overhead, softening the height of the ceiling and turning the space into something festive and intimate all at once.

Through the tall windows the gardens lie in twilight, lanterns glowing along the gravel paths where guests wander to get away from the fray for a moment or two.

At the center sits the cake. It's unapologetically spectacular. Four tiers of ivory buttercream are wrapped in delicate sugar flowers echoing the embroidery on Marisol's gown. Tiny, sparkly pearls along the edges catch the candlelight. It's art, not dessert.

I stand near Miranda with a glass of champagne, trying to behave like a normal human being instead of someone whose entire life has been upended in the best and most unexpected way.

Zach stands beside Julian and Irving near the bar. The three of them look almost identical in their midnight-blue tuxedos. Satin lapels. Crisp white shirts. Gold crown cufflinks glinting beneath the lights. Even Fred and Jose match them tonight.

Four generations of princes who wandered out of a Disney story.

Every few minutes his gaze lifts and finds mine, causing my heart to flip. I'm twenty-two again, sitting beside him in a lecture hall praying he thinks I'm pretty.

We haven't touched since the ceremony. Not because we don't want to. We promised each other to keep the focus where it belongs tonight. Marisol and Julian.

Before the reception began we slipped into the gardens for a breath of quiet between photographs and champagne. Zach turned toward me at the exact same moment I turned toward him.

"I told—"

"I told—" We spoke over each other.

"Julian and Irving," he admitted.

"Marisol," I replied.

For a second we stared at each other and let the absurdity settle in. Then we both started laughing.

"Well." He scrubbed a hand through his hair. "So much for subtle. Apparently we're terrible at secrets." He stepped a little closer, lowering his voice as guests began to filter into the ballroom again. "Maybe we behave for a few hours."

"Tonight belongs to them," I agreed.

For a little while longer, we'll let the celebration stay exactly where it belongs. Looking. Smiling. Not touching.

"Cake!" Soleil announces suddenly, her voice cuts through the music like a trumpet fanfare.

Sera appears beside her sister at the cake table with equal authority. The twins stand shoulder to shoulder. Tiny officials supervising the proceedings.

Julian and Marisol step forward, glowing in the afterlight of the ceremony. Cameras appear immediately. The guests gather around them in a loose half circle. The knife eases through the top tier. Applause breaks out.

Julian feeds Marisol the first bite with exaggerated ceremony. She retaliates with equal enthusiasm and nearly gets frosting on his lapel before rescuing the moment at the last second.

The twins cheer. Laughter reverberates while servers cut slices and pass them out.

Then someone taps a glass. "Toasts."

Fred goes first. His voice carries the warm steadiness of a man who has watched his son grow into himself over many years. He speaks about patience. About choosing a partner not just for joy but for the difficult days too.

Jose follows with stories about Marisol as a child. Stubborn, brilliant, determined even at eight years old she would have the perfect Disney wedding someday.

Then Irving rises. The law school friends brace for impact.

"Relax," he lifts his hands, "I promised the bride I'd behave."

No one believes him.

His speech opens with a story about Julian attempting to serenade Marisol outside the law school library with a borrowed guitar and exactly three chords.

Julian groans. Everyone else, including Marisol, roars with laughter. By the time Irving finishes, half the folks have tears in their eyes from laughing so hard.

Then Zach stands. The change in the atmosphere is immediate.

He doesn't rush to the center. He moves with the calm confidence he carries everywhere. He's always been the kind of man people listen to before he's even spoken.

He raises his glass. "Tradition says the best man should embarrass the groom," he begins.

"I see where this is going." Julian sighs loudly.

"Relax. I narrowed it down to three stories." Zach grins faintly. "Unfortunately none of them are appropriate for a room containing Marisol's mother."

Lupe lifts her glass in approval.

"So instead I'll tell you about the first time Julian told me he was in love with her."

Julian freezes. "Oh, jeez. You think you can trust your best friend..."

"We were twenty-two." Zach ignores him completely. "First year of law school. Julian came back from a study group in a daze. He sat across from me in the cafeteria and said—and I quote—'I think I just met the woman I'm going to marry.'"

Marisol covers her mouth. Julian groans again.

"And I said, 'You met her fifteen minutes ago.'"

Zach lifts one shoulder. "Turns out he was just seventeen years early."

Julian shakes his head while smiling helplessly.

"But here's the truth about these two," Zach continues once the laughter settles. "They built something most couples spend their lives trying to find."

He gestures at the twins. "They raised a family."

Toward the crowd. "They built friendships and a community stretching across continents."

Then back at Julian and Marisol. "Through every version of life. Law school. Careers. Kids. Everyday chaos. They never stop choosing each other."

A hush falls over the room.

"Most people stand here and promise a future." Zach holds up one hand. "Julian and Marisol are already living theirs. Today just makes it official." He lifts his glass. "To the bride and groom. May the next seventeen years be even better than the first."

Applause thunders, but Zach isn't finished.

He pauses.

Then his gaze lifts and finds mine across the crowd.

"One more thing," he adds.

My stomach drops.

"This wedding reminded me of something important."

Julian watches him carefully now.

"Life moves fast." Zach catches my eye and I can't look away. "You spend years focusing on your career. Building your reputation. Making money. Believing there's time to figure things out later. Then you realize the right person is standing in front of you and has been all along, you realize waiting was the worst decision you ever made."

All of my breath leaves my body.

"So if anyone here is still pretending they don't know who they're meant to be with—" His eyes stay locked on mine. "Take the fucking hint."

Julian laughs loudly.

I, on the other hand, am overwhelmed. He claimed me. In front of everyone. I know this because Zach watches me with quiet certainty and I'm positive every word was intentionally directed at me.

The music begins again. Julian and Marisol share a dance. Couples drift to the dance floor. I remain where I stand, holding my glass and trying to steady the rush of emotion rising in my chest.

Suddenly the joy of the evening carries a new weight. Zach and I are not a fantasy. This is turning into something real and the fear of what happens when the castle empties, the magic fades, and real life waits outside the gates is unavoidable.

I want to believe in the future he's promised, but I see firsthand how often fairy tales don't work out.

Can I believe in my own happily-ever-after?

Chapter Twenty

A Few Minutes Later

THE APPLAUSE AFTER MY toast rolls like a wave breaking against the stone walls.

For a moment I stay where I am at the podium, glass still in my hand, letting the moment settle.

Julian and Marisol kiss passionately. Sixty cheer. Laughter weaves through it. The band begins to play again somewhere behind me.

Good vibes everywhere.

Over by the bar—Sky.

She stands beside Miranda with her champagne glass hovering halfway to her lips. Watching me.

Good.

I lower the glass and start over.

People catch my sleeve as I pass. Fred claps me on the back hard enough to jostle my shoulder. Irving whistles because he's waited years for this exact moment.

None of it slows me down.

Sky doesn't move. She watches me walk over until I'm close enough to see the color in her cheeks.

"Hi." My eyes bore into hers.

Her laugh escapes before she can stop it. "Hi."

I slip my hands around her waist without hesitation, drawing her against me before either of us can retreat back into the careful restraint we've been practicing all evening.

"Zach—" Her eyes widen the moment she understands exactly what I'm about to do.

Because life is too short. Waiting is over.

For a heartbeat she looks up, eyes bright and breath suspended between surprise and surrender.

Then my mouth meets hers. A real fucking kiss. Not a careful version for the sake of the wedding.

Her lips part under mine. Warm from champagne. Sweet from frosting. The first slow brush sends heat through my chest. A spark catching dry wood. She inhales sharply, fingers clutching the lapels of my jacket as she pulls herself closer instead of stepping away.

Time and space disappear.

Sky's mouth opens to mine and I follow instinct, tilting slightly, letting the kiss deepen until her breath slips across my tongue and she answers with the same hunger. Her hand combs through my hair and curls around my nape, tugging gently. The small pull makes my heart ignite.

My palm spreads along the curve of her back, silk straining as I draw her closer.

Sky surges into me. Her mouth moves against mine with growing urgency, lips soft then firmer. Teeth graze my lower lip before she soothes the spot with a slow sweep of her tongue, sending a quiet jolt through my core.

Three sleepless nights flood back in fragments.

Fucking her senseless in my jet crossing the ocean. Burying myself inside her every night since. The sound of my name when she comes apart.

I chase the memory by kissing Sky harder. My tongue sweeps along the seam of her mouth and she welcomes me with a quiet gasp. A quiet mewl escapes her throat. Not meant for anyone else.

My thumb traces the soft skin of her chin while my other hand guides her closer until our bodies line up completely. She answers by rising slightly on her toes, lips moving faster against mine. Her tongue flicks lightly across mine before retreating, only to return again with playful insistence.

I answer with a slow sweep of my own. When we finally break the kiss she doesn't step away. Her forehead rests against mine while she catches her breath. I wrap my arms around her firmly.

After fifteen years of almost, letting go of Sky is no longer an option.

Ever.

Somewhere beyond the edge of the moment a sound breaks through. A low ripple of laughter. Then a whistle.

Sky freezes.

"Subtle." She brushes her thumb along my lip before glancing past my shoulder. "So this is how we're doing it now."

The reception hall rushes back into focus. Guests have turned in our direction. Glasses raised. Grins spreading across faces looking far more amused than shocked.

"Well," Irving's voice is thick with wicked amusement, "about damn time you two stopped pretending."

A smattering of laughter moves through the dancers.

Sky searches my face, equal parts stunned and delighted. "You realize, you made us the main event."

"Fifteen years." I keep her close enough to notice the quick rhythm of her breathing. "Marisol and Julian will understand. The moment was long overdue."

As if summoned by the thought, Julian and Marisol appear through the crowd.

His hand lands on my shoulder with a solid thump. "Finally."

"Oh thank God." Marisol steps beside him and her whole face lights up when she looks at Sky. "You two finally pulled your heads out of your asses."

Sky lets out a breathless laugh, pink spreading across her cheeks. "We weren't planning to make it a whole...moment. At your wedding. I'm so sorry."

"Sky, half the people in this room have been waiting for this since law school." Marisol takes her hands. "No thunder stolen. If anything, you gave everyone the ending we've all been hoping for."

Julian nods beside her, pointing between us. "Honestly, this might be the most predictable surprise in the history of weddings."

Sky glances at me again, relief and disbelief flickering across her face.

Behind her Irving appears looking smug. Or, a man preparing to deliver commentary to a jury.

"For the record," he raises his flute, "I'll remind Zach I encouraged this exact development including the red-eye rendezvous."

Sky closes her eyes briefly. "Please don't tell me..."

"Oh, I absolutely will." Irving tilts his head with unmistakable satisfaction. "I figured seven hours alone on a jet with one Skylar Morgan and he'd *finally* stop pretending."

"You said what?" Julian looks from Irving to me, eyebrows climbing.

Irving lifts one shoulder. "*Please*. I've been watching you two circle each other since Contracts." He raises one finger for emphasis. "Without my push, you'd still be in purgatory. My adjoining bedroom wall spent the last three nights confirming my theory."

"Please stop talking." Sky groans and hides her face briefly against my shoulder.

Irving only looks more pleased with himself. "I'm not even halfway through my victory lap."

"No, you leave them alone." Marisol bumps his arm aside. "They figured it out. That's the most important part."

Sky squints at me. "For fuck's sake. Apparently we've been very predictable."

I take her hand. "Only to people who know us best."

The band strikes up something upbeat and Julian grabs Marisol's hand. "Dance floor."

Within seconds the reception transforms into a full celebration. Chairs scrape back. Couples gather in clusters. The twins spin across the floor. Tween hurricanes in pale-blue dresses.

Sky looks at me, eyes bright. "Well, now we're out and proud. We might as well dance."

I take her hand. "Lead the way."

The next few hours dissolve into music and motion. The band plays everything from classic swing to ridiculous pop. Miranda drags Irving into a dance looking suspiciously like punishment. Fred attempts something resembling a waltz with Véronique while Jose cheers them on.

Sky and I rarely separate. Every time the music changes I pull her back into another turn. Eventually the band slows the tempo and we match the pace as the music softens. I ease my arm around her waist and bring her against me.

"Everyone is staring," she giggles.

"They've waited almost two decades for this. Let them enjoy it." I kiss her forehead.

She studies my face for a moment. "You seem very pleased with yourself."

"I am."

Her smile widens. "Good."

We sway slowly with the music while other guests move around us.

Behind us Irving's voice cuts through the quiet. "You know what this whole thing proves."

"Please stop," I growl.

Irving gestures dramatically. "Never underestimate the power of proximity and questionable decision-making on private aircraft."

"Oh my God." Sky laughs against my shoulder.

"Hey," Irving taps my shoulder, "I'm just saying. If every romance required a transatlantic jet and three sleepless nights, the divorce rate would plummet."

Sky shakes her head. "I can't him."

"You love it."

"I absolutely do."

Afterward, the night continues in waves. More dancing. Wine. Stories. An amazing night with friends and family. Hours pass without either of us noticing.

Eventually the band begins packing instruments. Guests drift toward the doors in laughing clusters.

Sky slips her hand into mine. "Ready?"

"Always." I lace my fingers through hers.

Together we leave the ballroom while the castle settles into night.

Chapter Twenty-One

Four Days Later

I WAKE SLOWLY, COCOONED in the warmth of Zach's body.

His arms encircle me and the unmistakable girth of his erection pushes against my bottom. Immediately, a familiar flutter of desire blooms deep inside me.

Apparently Prague agrees with us.

I rotate to snuggle him, smiling into the pillow as his arm grips instinctively around my waist. Even half-asleep, his body seems wired to keep me close. The sheets smell faintly of fresh linen and whatever decadent soap the Four Seasons stocks in its marble bathrooms.

The past four days are a dream I'm still reluctant to wake from.

The morning after the wedding we traded the castle for the city, letting the driver deliver us to the penthouse suite overlooking the Vltava River. The view alone nearly stole my breath. Terracotta rooftops stretched in every direction, cathedral spires piercing the skyline while the river curved lazily beneath Charles Bridge.

Zach walked straight to the windows, pulled me against his chest and declared, "We should stay here forever."

On the first day, we barely left the suite. It was something out of a glossy travel magazine. Cream-colored walls, dark wood floors, tall windows framed the river. Somewhere between unpacking and ordering room service, Zach discovered the oversized soaking tub.

Let's just say our plans for sightseeing were forgotten.

When we finally ventured out the following morning, it involved a Segway, which still makes me laugh.

Watching Zach Bennett, a six-foot-something corporate shark, wobble down a cobblestone street while a cheerful Czech guide explained how to incline forward nearly broke me.

"Don't laugh," he warned, gripping the handlebars.

"You're a very handsome mall cop," I told him.

We spent a couple hours gliding through Prague's winding streets, past pastel buildings and medieval towers, the Segways carrying us through quiet courtyards and narrow alleys where tourists hadn't yet crowded the morning. At one point we stopped on a hill by Prague Castle overlooking the city.

Zach tilted over and kissed me in front of the guide like he'd been doing it for years.

By evening we cleaned up for dinner at Benjamin.

The entire experience was a full-blown performance. At a specific time the dining room doors opened and the small group of guests were guided to their tables as if entering a private theater. Course after course arrived with quiet precision. Freshwater fish from nearby ponds. Foraged herbs scattered across delicate plates. Tender cuts of meat sourced from farms whose names were a roll call of the Czech countryside.

Each dish carried flavors I didn't recognize but somehow loved instantly.

Zach watched me like he was personally responsible for my pleasure. "I enjoy feeding you."

After dinner we walked back to our hotel across the Charles Bridge over the river as the city lights shimmered on the water.

And…well. Let's just say the penthouse bed has been thoroughly tested.

Which brings me back to the present moment.

I twist beneath Zach's arm. He stirs behind me.

"Morning," he murmurs, voice thick with sleep as his hand traces lazily along my hip.

He pulls me closer against him and his erection becomes far less subtle.

I laugh softly. "Apparently Prague agrees with you."

"Prague has excellent taste." He kisses the curve of my shoulder.

His hand snakes down to cup my breast, fingers teasing my nipple with gentle caresses, sending ripples of pleasure through my pussy. I instinctively arch my back, molding my butt to his thighs. He responds with a subtle thrust of his hips, causing the solid length of him to brush along the crease of my ass.

I turn my head to find his eyes dark and full of longing. I can't help but lean in for a kiss. The moment our lips meet, the kiss deepens, a delicious mingling of warmth and need.

Zach lifts my leg, positioning it over his, allowing the exquisite girth of his cock to nestle against my entrance. I can't help but gasp when he pushes inside, filling me completely. Always a perfect stretch. A fullness making me ache for him even more.

"God, you feel so good." Heat radiates from him, every inch sending electric shocks through my body.

"Keep going, I'm so close," I breathe, urging him on.

Each thrust is a deep, sensual dance where he skims against the sweet spot inside me, sending waves of pleasure radiating through my core.

I feel every pulse and it's intoxicating.

His fingers find my clit, rubbing in slow, deliberate circles. The sensations blend together. His cock gliding in and out, his fingers teasing my sensitive nub, and heat pools low in my belly. The tension is building, a slow simmer of arousal threatening to boil over.

"Zach, oh, yes. Please don't let up," I gasp, my hips instinctively moving to meet his thrusts, seeking more of the most delicious friction.

"You're so fucking sexy," he says, his voice laced with gravely lust. "Fucking you is heaven on earth. Your pussy is magic."

His tongue traces the curve under my ear, sending shivers down my spine. He pinches my nipple sharply, causing heat to coil tighter and tighter as he drives into me. Each thrust pushes me over the edge.

"Let go for me, baby," he urges. "Gush all over me."

Pressure builds, a sweet tension I'll never be able to live without again. His fingers continue to work my clit with expert precision, a combination of furious rubs and teasing flicks. He's driving me mad the way he plays my body.

"Zach, I'm so close," I moan, my fingers clutching at his arms, desperate for something to hold on to as I chase my peak.

"Come for me, Sky." His low, commanding tone pushes me to the brink.

With a final, powerful thrust, I tumble over the edge, my entire body convulsing in pleasure. "Oh God, yes!"

Waves of bliss crash over me. His cock pulses inside me, the warmth of his release mixes with the aftershocks of my own orgasm in a delicious swirl of sensation.

We stay connected, our bodies entwined as the world slowly comes back into focus.

"That was..." I start, but I can't find the words. Instead, I let my fingers trace along the defined muscles of his arm.

"Incredible?" he suggests, his eyes sparkling with mischief.

I snuggle in closer, feeling safe and cherished in his arms. "Better."

For a while we simply lie there, the quiet of the room. Prague wakes around us somewhere beyond the windows.

Zach's arm encircles me, a protective, certain yet unconscious gesture.

For years I've believed love is fragile. Something easily broken by time or distance or the ordinary complications of life.

Now, resting here with Zach, I realize my long-standing biases have loosened their hold.

Whatever comes next—Seattle, work, the thousand practical details waiting outside this room—we'll face it together.

For the first time in a long time, the future doesn't seem uncertain.

More like destiny.

ZACHARY

Epilogue - One Year Later

Morning in Poulsbo is quiet.

Water brushes the rocks below the bluff in a slow, steady rhythm. A gull crosses the pale sky beyond the window, its call drifting over the trees. The air carries a faint mix of salt and cedar.

I wake before Sky.

No alarm. Habit. My eyes open and settle on the woman beside me.

Sky sleeps curled against my side, one arm stretched across my ribs as if she fell asleep mid-sentence. Dark hair spills across the pillow in loose waves. Ever-present purple streak exactly where it belongs. The blanket has slipped low around her waist, revealing the gentle curve of her stomach.

Six months. My son growing inside her.

I roll onto my side, propping my head on my hand to study her while she sleeps. Her breathing stays slow and even. One of her feet rests against my calf.

A year ago my life was hotel suites and airplane cabins.

Now it's our cedar house on a hill overlooking an inlet on Puget Sound. A wide porch. Kitchen table permanently cluttered with notebooks, business plans, and whatever wild idea we're discussing the week. The beginnings of a nursery.

Sky stirs. Her fingers stiffen along my ribs before her eyes open halfway.

She blinks at me, still wrapped in sleep. She edges closer, resting her cheek on my chest. "You're awake."

"Been watching you sleep." I smooth the hair away from her face.

A small smile curves across her mouth.

"Romantic." Her hand drifts down to her stomach automatically, palm resting there with easy familiarity. The sleep shirt she slept in rides up, leaving a small strip of skin exposed.

I slide my hand across the sheet and cover hers. Movement answers beneath my palm.

Sky inhales softly. "There."

"He's kicking." My son moves against my hand.

She nods slowly, still smiling. "He's saying good morning, Daddy."

My thumb moves gently across the curve of her stomach. Another small kick follows, stronger this time.

"Feisty." A laugh escapes me.

Sky replies, pushing herself upright, "Your genetics."

The blanket shifts down as she moves, revealing the full curve of her belly.

Pride flickers across her face when she catches me looking. "You love this."

I kiss her warm skin. "Every second."

"You're going to be such a good dad." Sky runs her fingers through my hair in slow strokes.

"I'm practicing."

She laughs softly and swings her legs off the bed. The top falls loosely over her hips as she stands and stretches carefully. She goes to the window and pushes it open wider. Fresh air drifts inside.

"Doctor today," she glances over, "and the brewery meeting."

I nod. "We should leave by ten thirty."

Two women want to open a craft brewery down the road. Banks passed. We didn't. Turns out helping people build something meaningful is way better than chasing the next acquisition.

"You're really going to fund a brewery."

"Possibly."

Her smile grows. "Poulsbo suits you."

"It suits *us*." I reach over and lace my fingers through hers.

Her thumb moves slowly across my hand. Silence settles between us, easy and familiar.

Five months ago we stood in a neon chapel in Vegas laughing while an Elvis impersonator declared us husband and wife. Three weeks later Sky walked out of her law firm with a cardboard box and the calm certainty of a woman choosing a different life. Six weeks later, we heard our son's heartbeat for the first time.

Everything changed.

We're living our best life.

Sky rotates in her chair and pulls my hand back to her stomach. Another small kick answers.

Her eyes meet mine. "He's awake again."

I caress her belly. Fluttery movement causes a slow grin to spread across my face.

Sky giggles. "You're completely gone."

"I've been gone for years."

Outside the window the water moves in quiet silver lines across the inlet.

Sky squeezes my hand once.

Together, the road ahead is simple.

Inevitable.

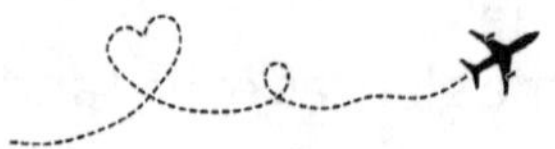

Thank you for reading *Red Eye Rendezvous*. If Skylar and Zachary's second chance meant something to you, I'd love it if you left a quick review: Leave your review here.

The journey doesn't end here. If you want more from the *Hearts Without Borders* world, join me here for sneak peeks, behind-the-scenes moments, and first access to everything still to come.

Want to know where Skylar's story begins in the LTZ world? Keep reading for the epilogue from *Hushed Harmony*.

Behind the Scenes

PRAGUE LIVES IN MY heart in a way few cities do, so when I started writing these travel novellas, I knew Prague would be part of the series.

My *Hearts Without Borders* series gives me a chance to revisit places I love and share them through characters discovering something life-changing at the same time.

Sky and Zach belonged here.

If you read *Hushed Harmony*, you met Sky already. She stepped in as the brilliant attorney who helped Liam, Avonna, and Linus protect their unconventional family. Three people deeply in love needed someone smart enough to build legal guardrails around their life together.

She also carried her own complicated beliefs about love, which made her perfect for a friends-to-lovers story.

I adore this trope. Especially when two people stay friends for years ignoring their attraction to each other out of fear. Everyone around them sees the sparks and patiently waits for them to pull their heads out of their asses (I think someone may have said this exact line...).

Also... I need to admit something.

I love the 80's movie *St. Elmo's Fire*. The music, the friendships, the way a tight group of college friends grow up together and stay tangled in each other's lives long after graduation.

Hopefully you're catching the vibe I'm throwing down.

Years of shared history. Brutal honesty. Deep loyalty. Friends who see the truth before the two people involved finally catch up.

As far as Prague goes, if you ever have the chance to visit, go. Walk Charles Bridge early before the tour groups arrive. Wander Old Town Square and look up at buildings painted in colors you rarely see anywhere else. Eat a long dinner somewhere tiny and wonderful where the chef cares deeply about every ingredient on the plate.

Let yourself get lost in the streets—especially on a Segway. TRUST!

These little travel novellas give me a way to revisit places that changed me. I'm excited to bring readers along for the ride.

Thank you for spending time with Sky and Zach.

Stay tuned for the next!

Hushed Harmony

LIAM

Prologue – Present Day

I SHOULDN'T HAVE COME.

This was the conversation I had with myself on the flight.

And again, when the taxi crossed river Liffey and the Dublin skyline came into view.

I've never been here. This is a city I've spent years avoiding. Until a few months ago, my band Fireball had never played in Ireland at all. I made sure of it. Always found a reason to avoid it.

Too many ghosts.

Too much history I wasn't ready to deal with.

A few days ago, Linus messaged.

Simple. Polite.

```
Linus: If you're passing through
Dublin when you're done with the
European tour, maybe let's talk.
```

Fuck.

I've spent what seems like a million years chasing the rockstar dream with my twin brother Padraig. Living out of vans. Crashing on floors. Putting out music. Bleeding for every gig. He should've walked years ago to follow the girl he loved. He didn't because I needed him to stay.

I live with the guilt every fucking day.

Our once-close family is a mess. After a car accident, Da turned into a bitter, misogynistic drunk. Gambled the family money. Drove the business into the ground.

Oh, and he nearly killed me.

Apparently, none of this was bad enough for my ma to leave him.

My oldest brother Connor gave up everything when the old man went down. Quit college. Took over the business. Raised the rest of my brothers like a second father. Now he's the bass player in Less Than Zero, the biggest band in the world.

This summer, he gave Fireball a much-needed boost by giving us the opening time slot on their European tour. We were able to fill in the gaps with a slew of festival gigs.

We killed it, but in true Fireball form our lead singer quit and now we're back to the fucking drawing board.

Once again, the band is teetering. Padraig won't say the words, but I see it in his eyes. He's almost out.

He's always followed my lead, trusting my determination to make us a success even when he's wanted something else. Now, we're back to square one, and he may not have it in him to continue.

I don't blame him. Without a stable front person, we're probably chasing something already dead.

The thing is, I've poured my entire life into this band and can't give up on us yet. Abandoning the only steady thing I've ever had isn't an option.

I understand loss. I've fucked my way around the world to try to quell the grief. Men. Women. Whatever would help me forget the only person I've ever given my heart to.

Linus O'Donnell.

My college love. He managed the band. Believed in us and the music when few others did. We were working our way up when his visa expired and he returned home to Ireland. I didn't ask him to stay. Fight for him when it counted.

At the time, I convinced myself I didn't deserve to have love when my brother gave up his.

I've purposely stayed away as both penance and punishment.

Until now.

Goddammit.

He's gonna break me all over again.

I'm a self-destructive motherfucker.

It's the end of the business day. I'm sitting in a café in the heart of the city, I pretend the coffee in front of me is worth drinking. The place is quiet, warm, and full of people typing or reading or staring at their phones. My leg won't stop bouncing.

The door opens.

Linus steps in, shakes off the drizzle, looks around and spots me instantly.

He glides through the room like temptation in human form. Button-down snug across his chest, sleeves rolled barely enough to expose the tattooed edges of his forearms. Slacks hug his hips like they are a custom fit. His dark hair is longer now and a thick beard covers his square jaw.

He doesn't try to be hot. He just is. My cock stiffens the second I see him.

Always has. Always will.

When he catches my eye and smiles, tentative and crooked, my stomach lurches.

I'm done for.

He walks over, calm as ever, and I stand without thinking.

"Liam."

"Hey."

He slides into the seat across from me and sets his phone face down on the table. No handshake. No small talk. Unflappable fucking composure, considering.

For an impossibly long moment, neither of us speaks.

Two grown men pretending we don't remember how it felt to share air like this. To frot our cocks together, desperate and leaking. To love each other so fiercely it nearly destroyed both of us.

He breaks first. "You look tired, so you do."

"Tour ended yesterday." I lean back and cross my arms protectively over my chest.

"Youse headin' home soon?"

"A few days." I relax a bit. "Padraig's up at Connor's new Belfast estate. Helpin' him get it ready for his famous girlfriend."

He nods. "Wow. An estate in Belfast. Sounds like a true rockstar move."

"Aye." I look out the window. It's challenging to maintain eye contact with the one man who owns you.

Silence again.

I glance at his hands. Strong. Capable. Once they explored every part of my body. "Congratulations, by the way. Seems like you're livin' the dream. Isis Management's a big deal."

"Thank you, it's doing well. Movin' operations to LA soon." He doesn't take his goddamn eyes off me. We both know we're not here to talk business.

"Avonna seems to be the magic sauce." I don't mean to bring up his client and I certainly don't mean for it to come out so sexual. Like I'm already thinking about her mouth on my cock.

But hell. I am who I am.

The woman is a fucking knockout. Voice like velvet and razorblades. The deep pain behind her eyes makes you wanna fuck her and protect her in the same breath. She played a few of the same festivals with us this summer. Lit the place on fire and walked off stage like it was routine.

She's unreal. Exactly my type.

"She is." He smirks. He knows exactly what I'm thinking. "One of the best voices I've ever heard."

"I agree." I nod too enthusiastically. "She's special."

"Aye. Special," he repeats, eyes fixed on me. "You like her."

It isn't a question.

I shift in my seat. "Well sure, she's talented."

"Not what I meant." He leans forward slightly, studying my face.

I stare into my cup. "You want honesty?"

"Always."

"Yeah. I'm attracted to her. Probably too much. We had some good chats on the road." I think back to the handful of times she and I had an opportunity to visit in between our sets.

What I don't say is, other than the man in front of me, she's the only other person I've instantly connected with on an otherworldly level.

"Do you wanna fuck her?" The words hit like a punch.

I choke on the air in my throat. "Jesus, *Linus.*"

"Do you?" His gaze doesn't waver.

I drag a hand through my hair. "Fer fuck's sake. You manage her. She's magnetic. Gorgeous. I can't be the only one."

"There's a lot more to Avonna than what men want from her." He clasps his fingers together and leans forward.

Instantly, I feel like a dick. "Uh...I know. I, uh, didn't mean..."

"Why'd you come here, Liam?" He stares into my eyes.

I hold his gaze, heart pounding. "You asked."

Emotions flicker across his face. Surprise. Relief. Pain.

I exhale. "We saw each other a few times this summer. You barely spoke to me. When you texted, I couldn't ignore it this time."

"Liam. I've reached out *dozens* of times over the years." He winces, finally showing his emotional cards. "You ignored every outreach."

"I know." I scrub my chin with my fist and cast my eyes down.

His jaw wobbles. "I thought we meant somethin'."

"We meant everything."

"You broke me." He shakes his head, more weary than angry.

The words land heavy. I don't try to deny them. "I broke me too."

The quiet between us strains with everything unsaid. Dozens of people bustle past the window. Somewhere behind the counter, an espresso machine hisses.

I meet his eyes. "I'm sorry."

"For which part?" Linus leans back and folds his arms.

"All of it."

He shakes his head. "Do you think saying sorry fixes it?"

"No."

"Then why bother?"

"It's true."

He studies me for a long time, like he's trying to find the man he used to love inside the one sitting across from him. Maybe he regrets inviting me to Dublin. Maybe he hopes I'll walk out the door and never look back.

Maybe he's daring me to stay.

"I hated you for givin' up on us," he says finally.

"I know."

He swallows. "Still do, some days."

"I deserve it."

He nods. "Aye. You do."

We sit there for another prolonged silence. Two ghosts in a city filled with history and war and heartbreak far worse than ours. I don't know what I thought this would be. Closure? Forgiveness? Maybe I wanted proof he and I were once real.

When he finally speaks again, his voice is softer. "You didn't have to come."

"I did," I insist. "You invited me."

"Curiosity isn't the same as closure." He bites his lip, probably to avoid saying more.

I call his bluff. "Well, then, why did you text?"

He holds my gaze for a long time, something shifts behind his expression.

Hurt. Longing. Restraint.

"I wanted to see if there's anything left."

"And?" My blood pressure spikes.

He arches an eyebrow. "Still figurin' it out."

We both laugh under our breath. It's not funny, but it's real.

"I've missed this," I admit.

He looks down. "Which part?"

"All of it."

This earns me the faintest smile. Gone before I can memorize it.

Outside, the rain gets heavier. Inside, it feels like we're both teetering at the edge of something we never finished. Neither of us moves to leave. Neither of us asks for more coffee.

We sit here in a buffalo stance. Two versions of the same wound.

I shouldn't have come.

But, realistically, I never had a choice

Linus thankfully changes the subject. "So. How's Padraig?"

I glance out the window. "Same. One foot in, one foot gone. He swears he's quittin' every six months, but he never does."

"Still loyal."

"Still pissed."

"At you?"

I shake my head. "At himself."

Linus watches me, unreadable. I go on. "He had everything once. A great love. Someone to grow old with. Now he's only got me and a rockstar dream he never wanted."

"Not true. He always intended on doing this with you." He nearly reaches for my hand, but visibly restrains himself.

"It's complicated," I concede. "He loves makin' music with me but doesn't enjoy the rest of it. The grind. The instability. We've lost three singers. Koko was the best of them. She lasted the longest."

Linus tilts his head. "So, it's true? Is she really gone?"

"Yep. Left after the last show." I wince. "Got a solo deal."

"Timing is terrible. You're finally on the mainstream charts." Linus furrows his brow.

"Yeah, well, she wants her own thing. Said the band didn't feel sustainable."

"Is it?"

I let out a bitter laugh. "Depends who you ask. To me, Fireball is all I've dreamed of. To Padraig, it's all he's got. Truthfully, we're taking a short break to regroup."

Linus nods slowly. "Wow. Heavy."

"Yeah."

"Will he walk away?"

"Ach, no. Probably not on his own accord." I keep my eyes fixed on Linus' strong hands before I flick my eyes up to his. "Maybe I should let him."

He doesn't answer. He doesn't have to.

Then he says, carefully, "So you're in Dublin to patch holes."

I exhale. "Aye. I suppose I am."

The shift is subtle, but I feel it. The weight of everything unsaid pulls the air tighter between us.

Things we didn't finish. Lingering feelings.

I remember the last time I touched him. Boarding pass in his hand. My heart clogged with grief. The frantic way he kissed me. Held me so tightly like he never wanted to let go.

Now we're here. The past bleeding forward, asking if we still matter.

We do.

God, we do.

I feel the tether between us. Tenser than it has any right to be.

He finishes his coffee and leans back. "I'm a few blocks away."

I nod.

He doesn't say come over. He stands, trusting I'll follow.

I do.

We walk without touching. Like our bodies are afraid of remembering too fast.

By the time we get to his building, I don't know if I want to kiss him or punch him.

Maybe both.

He opens the door, steps aside to let me in.

I cross the threshold and feel it. The weight of the years. Breath catching before something breaks.

I turn toward him.

Neither of us speaks.

It's not awkward.

It's inevitable.

You've seen what's waiting. Now start at the beginning with Hushed Harmony.

Acknowledgments

Cover Design: Kate Farlow Y'all. That Graphic.
Editor: Grace Bradley Editing, LLC
Formatting: Willow Yanarella
PR: Dani Sanchez Wildfire Marketing
Literary Agent: Stephanie Phillips, SBR Media
Website Maven: Sherri Kiarsis, Ruby Moon Designs
My Right Hand: Willow Yanarella
Can't forget about Anna Theurer, not only one of my PAs, she has been with me since the beginning.
YAY to Kaylene's Backstage Krew, my wonderful ARC Team!

Dedication

For my husband, my favorite travel partner and the one who proves every day the best stories aren't the ones we write, they're the ones we live.

About the Author

KAYLENE WINTER IS A best-selling author of steamy, contemporary romance.

Each character-driven novel is filled with snappy dialogue, pop-culture references and enough steam to make you fan yourself. Kaylene weaves authenticity, emotion and angst into a turbulent rollercoaster ride of love, passion and soul-searing romance always ending with a delicious HEA.

Kaylene lives in Seattle with her amazing Irish husband and her Pomsky, Phalen. She loves creating art of all kinds.

Other Titles